DON JUAN
IN THE VILLAGE

other novels by jane delynn:

Real Estate

In Thrall

Some Do

DON JUAN
IN THE VILLAGE

A NOVEL

jane delynn

PANTHEON BOOKS   NEW YORK

Library of Congress Cataloging-in-Publication Data
DeLynn, Jane.
  Don Juan in the village : a novel / Jane DeLynn.
    p. cm.
  ISBN 0-394-58691-3
  I. Title.
PS3554.E4465D66   1990
813'.54—dc20   90-52559

Book Design by Anne Scatto
Manufactured in the United States of America
First Edition

for m.c.

contents

acknowledgments

I'd like to thank the staff and Corporation of Yaddo, where much of the first draft of the novel was written, and the New York Foundation for the Arts, for its useful and timely grant. I would also like to thank my literary agent, Eric Ashworth, for his patience and support, and my editor, Helena Franklin, for her enthusiasm, perceptiveness, and relentless attention to detail.

DON JUAN
IN THE VILLAGE

the waif

I was trying to survive. Every night was a torment to me during which I prayed God not to let me jump out of the window and kill myself. I would turn on the television, take a pill, and try to sleep. Often in the day I was so tired my head would fall forward at my desk or even on the subway and I would fall asleep sitting up. A book or newspaper would fall out of my hand, but I would wake up quickly enough to catch it before it fell. And in this tiny fraction of a second many thoughts would go through my head, and I would congratulate myself on my reflexes and the quickness of my brain.

It had kept up like this for many days when I went to The Bar. I could never quite decide if going to The Bar made me feel better or worse, and until I had made this decision there was no reason not to go. Even when there was no one I was attracted to, more than likely I would run into someone I knew; if I didn't, I could absolutely count on the music, the clank of glasses, the familiar conversations, the glint of bottles and faces in the mirror suspended over the bar, both to distract me and—since I had spent so many hours there—to remind me of myself.

On seeing me, Monica walked over. She was from Germany, but as she was dark and fashionably dressed I thought of her not as "German" but as "European," which helped defuse the question of national prejudice. Oddly, though I detest Germany and everything it stands for, I can usually tolerate individual Germans.

In Monica's wake trailed a woman: a girl really, thin and pale, the kind one would once have called tubercular. She was just Monica's type, but for some reason girls that were just Monica's type never liked her. Well, I suppose each of us knew the reason: Monica was both overweight and too clever. I am clever too, but not heavy, and in recent years I have learned to handle my cleverness better.

I bought the waif a beer, then another. I couldn't tell whether she liked me or was so broke she just wanted me to buy her a drink. I watched her carefully in the hope of finding out whether her drunkenness was habitual or merely a product of this evening. It was impossible to tell, so I whispered the question to Monica.

"What are you talking about?" the waif asked suspiciously.

"She's asking me how I could let someone as attractive as you get away," said Monica, as if making a joke. The girl shrugged, then looked across the room. She looked about eighteen, but she was probably twenty-one. They're very strict about age in the bar now; it's one of the violations commonly used to close us down.

It had been late when I arrived, and after a few beers hardly anyone was left, at two-thirty on even a Saturday—okay, Sunday morning. Then Monica was saying goodnight, and I realized the waif was waiting for me to invite her home. I assumed that for some reason—perhaps a fight with a lover—she had nowhere to sleep.

The waif was too drunk for me to try to impress her with a big taxi tip, so I decided to give a normal one. Then the thought of my having thought about this disturbed me—both in the moral and the esthetic sense—so I ended up giving a large one after all. Both my building and my apartment clearly impressed her. I opened a bottle of beer and handed it to her. She was too drunk to drink it but it gave her something to play with while I walked around the apartment, turning the music up, the lights down, and so on. Finally I sat next to her on the couch. She was so thin and pale I decided I did not find her attractive after all. Or perhaps I did, but I was awfully tired. As soon as I decided this, I felt sorry for her and put my arm around her and drew her to me out of a sense of guilt and obligation. I didn't want her to realize I didn't find her so attractive.

We went into the bedroom. She lay down on the bed. She passed out or perhaps pretended to pass out, I couldn't tell. In any case, whether she knew it or not, it was okay. I took off her shoes and unzipped her pants. She wasn't wearing underpants under her jeans. This was rare enough that it should have been more of a turn-on, but what I kept thinking was that unless she washed her jeans every day or so they would start to smell—and nobody washed their jeans every day. I thought of checking them to find out, then I decided I didn't want to know. She herself did not have a bad smell so I lay with my head on her stomach a long time debating about whether or not I should go down on her. Not for her sake but for my own. Although I was very tired my mind was racing from alcohol and I felt I would be unable to fall asleep unless I partook of this soothing activity. Years ago, when the picking up of women in bars was still an astounding novelty for me, I had found it difficult to fall asleep next to these exciting strangers, and this sleeplessness reminded me not of my current insomnia, but of the kind from that long ago and happier time. This feeling did not bring me closer to that time but made it seem even farther away, like the memory of a book read in childhood. At this moment, on the edge of forty, I would have traded all those nights for one living human being, say ten or twelve years old, the child I would doubtless never have.

Sunday afternoon the waif told me her story. I had taken her to brunch at a casual but chic café down the block from me. I asked her questions as she dutifully ate her food. She seemed to acknowledge the necessity for food without actually liking it. She had been living with an older woman who was alcoholic, abusive, a real monster. Two weeks ago she had come from Virginia to stay with a friend; then last night this friend and she had had a fight. She had no money and no job. She was twenty-two. She hadn't gone to college. As we ate I kept trying to decide whether or not I was attracted to her. I finally came to the conclusion she was attractive but that for some reason I was not especially turned on by her, though perhaps this would change. I told her she could stay with me if she wanted.

We bought a paper and returned to my apartment. She put on a record and I turned on the television, but with the volume low so I could watch the football game without sound. My fatigue caught up with me as I tried to read and I kept nodding off. I was so tired I did not stop myself from draping an arm around her. She let it lie there as she read another section of the paper. I would drift off and wake up to find her still reading the paper, my arm still around her neck. At a certain point I realized my arm had gone numb from pain and I moved it. I didn't know what to do with it so I withdrew it and laid my head down on her lap. The next time I woke up I realized I was drooling on her jeans. I looked up at her. She looked at me, smiled, pushed the hair off my forehead with her fingers.

She fit very well into my routine. I could work as well as if she weren't there—better, really, since I felt less need to go out. Soon I would have to inform my friends of my new situation, but in the meantime I enjoyed it as an amusing secret. Often I fantasized conversations in which I would tell my friends about her: "We never talk. I don't even know her last name . . ." Of course I knew her last name, but not much more. I knew she hated her mother and that she had several brothers and sisters whose names I could never keep straight, most of whom were born-again Christians. Once she had loved a friend in high school, but nobody since. The only time she had ever kissed this friend was in the car at some high school dance, while they were waiting for their boyfriends. They were drunk and the next time she tried something her girlfriend told her she was sick. They had never discussed the incident again.

In turn I told her stories about women I had been with; it was the only subject I could think of to talk to her about. "You seem to have loved an awful lot of people," she said. Usually I think of myself as a cold and unfeeling person, but I realized now that what she said was true. But when I tried to count them it was oddly difficult. Depending on who and what I included—women I thought I had loved but had never slept with, women I had not gotten enough of and continued to yearn for, women I had slept with so often I had felt obliged rather than compelled to use the word "love"—it was somewhere between five and twenty. For a moment I felt proud of this number, a real Don Juan, then sadness welled up at the thought of all the hours—years, really—I had spent dreaming about women who hadn't loved me back, who would have been astonished to learn of the energy and time that had been emotionally invested in them, whose phone numbers I had dialed merely so I could hear their irritated voice demanding "Who *is* this?" whose apartment buildings I had detoured past in the hope of bumping into them as they brought home bags of groceries or laundry that I could help them carry up the stairs. Even should I meet someone this very night with whom I would live in perfect bliss for the rest of my life, I could never make up for those past miseries, perhaps the most intense of which occurred when I was in high school, twenty-odd years ago. . . . Then a thought that had heretofore managed to escape me—that there might be women out there who had suffered on my account the same way I had suffered for others, who had waited at home (in those long-off days before the invention of the answering machine), scared to go out lest I should call, women who had spent miserable nights walking around their apartments, conducting endless dialogues with me in their heads, pounding on their pillows, calling upon God to rescue them from the utter misery of their yearnings—occurred to me, and tears of pity for these possibly imaginary beings welled up in my eyes. Amidst such depressing thoughts, I fell asleep.

Eventually it was time to include the waif in my life. We stopped going to movies alone, and began to have dinner with my friends. She didn't say much of anything. In the beginning I worried constantly about whether she was bored, then I decided the only way I could achieve peace was by not worrying about it. Whenever the thought crossed my mind I would deliberately push it away. It was clear she did not especially enjoy sex with me, and initially this was enough to prevent me from trying anything with her, unless I was especially horny or so high from beer or marijuana that I was no longer concerned about what she was feeling. On the other hand, with the exception of one or two occasions, she did not specifically reject me, and I told myself that surely I could be no more displeasing to her than that horrible woman in Virginia she had run away from. Gradually I developed an assumed indifference to her feelings which I was sure would hold me in good stead in the future. By this I don't mean I didn't use all the resources at my command to try and transport her to regions of bliss. I don't mean just expertise, but the

knowledge I had gained from experience, the basic intu-
itiveness of my feelings, and—not least—the energy I had
always been willing to expend on such activities. Of course
my ego had to be involved in such matters; how much I
wasn't sure. I decided it wasn't necessary for me to know.
In my head I told myself I loved her. I told her I loved
her all the time, so much so it bored her. I think perhaps
I said it to bore her. I wondered how I would respond if
she ever told me she loved me. Remembering other such
moments, I told myself surely it would not be as wonderful
as I supposed. Of course, there seemed little danger of
this. She never said anything about me or her feelings for
me, except that I was "very nice." For some reason this
pleased me inordinately, and in my head I replayed the
scene where she had told me this all the time. She had
been sitting on the couch. A newspaper was in her lap. It
was late afternoon. She had patted my head. In my
giddiness I knocked over a cup of cold coffee that was
sitting on the floor. I started to get up, but she told me
no, not to disturb myself, that she would take care of it
herself. I'm not sure, but I believe tears came to my eyes.

Usually during the day she went out—"just to walk
around," as she put it. Sometimes she mentioned friends
she had seen. When I asked to meet them she said I
wouldn't be interested in them. When I asked her where
she had met them she said, "Oh, you know, here and
there." The first thing she did in the morning was roll a
joint and smoke it. Initially I tried to keep up with her,
then I realized it was interfering with my work, so for the
most part I stopped. She told me one of her friends was
a dealer and always gave her some. I assumed she, too,
was dealing in a small-time way, but I let it pass. I was

glad she was smoking harmless marijuana instead of doing something expensive and dangerous like coke.

It's possible things would have continued this way forever if my friend Jan had not returned to town. Certain friendships are reciprocal; in others, one person makes all the moves. That's how it was with Jan and me. It was not that I disliked her or even was particularly bored in her presence; it's just that there never seemed any particular reason to call her. Even though we had been friends for years, I was always surprised and a little flattered by her calls, as I always am by the attentions of attractive and relatively unintelligent people with whom I have little or nothing in common.

Jan wore too much makeup and jewelry. She did most of the talking in our relationship, though much of it was only to ask for advice. She rarely took it, but this didn't stop her from asking me, or me from giving it; I guess I enjoyed lecturing her. She must have enjoyed being lectured to, too; perhaps this was the basis of our relationship. Her problem was either she liked women who didn't like her, or when women liked her she didn't like them, or when she met someone whom she liked, that person had just moved in with someone else, or if by chance the woman was living by herself it was someplace far across the continent or maybe even in some other country entirely. I would point out to Jan that this happened too frequently for it to be mere coincidence, which she would attempt to refute via some long story purporting to prove that *this* time, unlike all the others, there were mitigating circumstances that for once even I would have to allow.

"Even I": as if I were a cruel (or even caring) observer. Perhaps it was my physical indifference to her that intrigued her; she simply was not my type, though women similar to her often were.

From the very first Jan and the waif got on extremely well. The waif would perk up at Jan's stories, even laugh, the way she rarely did at mine. They began to go to bars together, nights I preferred to stay home and work. The first time I did this to test my jealousy, but the waif came back early enough, not especially drunk, and I noticed I had enjoyed the time without her. Gradually I came to welcome these expeditions. I asked myself which of them I'd be angrier at if the waif left me for Jan. In great detail I worked out the scene in my head. It did not cause me much pain and I decided that perhaps it would be all to the good: Jan was nearer the waif in age than I was and they really had much more in common. *Que será será.* Perhaps as a result, I had never felt so peaceful in a relationship. I would say I was happy too, but usually I reserve that word for that peculiar state of desire one can have only for those one does not lie next to in bed every night. As long as the waif was there it was not necessary to desire her.

One night she did not come home. By one-thirty I was so upset that all pretense of work or reading was a joke. I decided it was beneath my dignity to call Jan. I lived with this decision as long as I could, then I called someone in California who I knew would still be awake. We talked till five A.M. New York time, past the hour when bars close, when even a drunken or stoned walk should have brought the waif back to me. Finally the sleeping pill I had taken during this conversation kicked in, and I was able to get off the phone and go to sleep.

The waif woke me with a phone call at ten-thirty the next morning. After leaving the bar she had walked Jan home. It was still early so she had gone upstairs with her to smoke a joint. The stuff was unusually strong, like the stuff we had had the night we went to that hot new club in Chelsea. By the time she began to come down and realized what time it was, it was nearly four. She was too tired to walk home and didn't have the money for a taxi. Nor did she want to telephone and wake me up. "How come you don't mind waking me up now?" I asked. "How come you didn't ask Jan for money for a taxi?" She told me she'd be home shortly; then she hung up.

I tossed and turned in bed waiting for her. I figured she'd be there within half an hour, surely an hour. But two, then three hours went by. Eventually I got up. During the course of the day I rehearsed various scenes in my head, some having to do with last night, others having to do with the morning's phone call and my having waited in bed for her, but by the time she arrived shortly before dinner I had so exhausted them that the emotions behind them had lost all potency. Dully I made supper. She turned on the TV and leafed through the *Post*. Once or twice, as was her habit, she read a little tidbit or two from Page 6 which amused her. Usually I liked this, but now I exploded. "Don't you think you can get out of this by trying to be charming," I shouted at her.

"Get out of what? I told you, nothing happened." Calmly

she went back to the paper. By the end of dinner somehow my anger had evaporated. More than dissipated, it had turned into a peculiar sort of lightheartedness. The thought of someone I was totally supporting cheating on me—and so casually—was not without its comic side. I felt like a protagonist in a novel by Colette. The more I put up with it, the more it would serve to distance me in her mind from that monstrous woman in Virginia, her cold and unsympathetic mother, all the terrible teachers and Girl Scout leaders and camp counselors who had oppressed her during the course of her unhappy life.

She did not shower before we got into bed that night. I smelled her to see if she had bathed at Jan's. She didn't smell fresh, but then she wasn't acrid either, so I found it impossible to tell. In general she was a person remarkably free of odor. I liked her so much I smelled good around her too—something which, when you think about it, isn't always the case.

The TV was on. I slid down her body and laid my head on her pale thighs. Never had I known anyone with so little hair. With a total lack of desire I began to lick her. I could have been a chimpanzee grooming myself, so completely without reference to passion of any sort were my actions. She lay with her legs spread, indifferent as always, watching TV. Even though the picture was behind my back I could follow what was happening just by listening. For a long time I kept my eyes open, but eventually I closed them. Again I thought about her and Jan. The thought did not arouse me but the fact that it no longer made me upset in any way astonished me. The comedy changed to a comedy-drama, then a cop show. I realized I had been doing this an awfully long time. During the comedy and the comedy-drama her breathing had been slow and regular as it always was. I was so used to this it didn't bother me; if anything, I was disconcerted and almost displeased when during the cop show it began to speed up. At first I assumed this had to do with something exciting happening in the plot, which I only then realized I had stopped paying attention to—but no, the accelerated breathing continued even during the advertisements. I was so tired from the worrying of the night before, I kept pulling myself awake with a start. I couldn't tell whether I had fallen asleep for half a second or for a much longer period of time. In any case, whenever I woke up I would recommence my activities. She did not seem to notice any change, so probably it was just for a moment, like when I would catch the book falling from my hands at my desk or on the subway. And yet in that brief half-second it seemed as if I had been dreaming—but perhaps ordinary time also is suspended for dreams. Initially when her breathing became faster and more audible, I thought this too was part of my dream. Then I realized I was awake, and that my sleepy absentmindedness was causing a re-action that all my conscious desires and energy and ex-perience had for so long failed to do. Perhaps this was due to my sleepiness and indifference, or my fantasies concerning her and Jan, perhaps merely on account of the TV programs, which more than once I had seen dredge tears from her simple heart. When at last she came she lay silent a long time, then she told me it was the first time. I felt flattered and rather proud, as if a daughter of mine had graduated with good marks from high school.

She told me it had been less thrilling than she had been led to expect, and asked me if that was all.

"Yes," I told her, that was all. She was silent a long time, then, relieved perhaps, or merely indifferent, she tried, also for the first time, to work a similar magic on me.

puerto rico

One of the things I like to do when I travel is fraternize with the natives, and of the many ways to do this, sex is perhaps the best. You can walk down the streets, of course, and follow a person dressed in a certain style in the hope they will lead you to a certain kind of place, but it is easier and far more certain to buy a guidebook—a guidebook for special persons of special tastes. It will supply you with the names and locations of bars around the world, and something of the kind of person and experience you are likely to encounter in these bars. There are guides for men and women—and no doubt for some of the other sexes too.

I was staying by myself in a guest house in the Condado

area of San Juan. Although it was a guest house for persons of special tastes, which I had been told would be good for someone who was traveling on her own, I found it extremely difficult to engage anybody in conversation. This was a while ago, after people like us had gotten over the initial excitement of beginning to talk about ourselves and our condition both to ourselves and to the world outside, but when we were still supposed to be kindly disposed towards each other—not just women and women, or men and men, but women and men as well—and the lack of friendliness there surprised me. Disillusionment had already begun to set in, a disillusionment similar to that in love when you realize that the two who thought they were one are really two after all, but a kind of consensus was around whose intent was maybe not so much to hide this realization as to pretend it was not important. The more we hid it, of course, the more important it became, but I had made efforts to overcome my natural cynicism concerning the possibility of change in the behavior and attitudes of human beings towards one another, and I was not yet willing to admit that these efforts had been in vain.

I suspect that this is too sophisticated an analysis of the situation, that in fact I was at a place and with people who had never been particularly interested in the initial excitement I'm referring to, who therefore would not have suffered any disillusionment, whose friendliness or lack of it was less a matter of consensus than of simple preference. Quite possibly these were people who refused to admit they were different from the world around them; very likely they were people who refused to discuss the subject at all. I couldn't tell, I could only guess, because nobody was talking to me. Most of the people not talking to me were Americans, but people from other parts of the island or the Caribbean were managing to ignore me too.

One problem was I was the only woman traveling alone. Even if the others were not in couples, they were part of a group. Although this happened constantly, somehow I never managed to anticipate it; I kept expecting to encounter other solo adventurers similar to me in everything but hair color. I wondered why it had been suggested I come here, to that part of the Caribbean which most resembles Miami Beach. I would stroll down the Condado looking at the big hotels and their kidney- or heart-shaped pools with intense disgust, wishing I were on a tiny island with straw huts whose thatched roofs leaked in the rain. I felt contempt for the women and men sitting around the pools with triangles of aluminum-covered cardboard under their chins reflecting the sun onto their faces as they drank pineapple daiquiris and listened to Gloria Gaynor singing "I Will Survive" on their ghetto-blasters. These were the years before Walkman, and disco was big then; for the first time in my life I swam to a beat. Perhaps it was appropriate; I was swimming in a city. The swimming didn't calm me; it only set me up for the things of night.

The guidebook suggested several bars where tourists might feel welcome, but since I travel so as not to be me, I decided on a local bar, a place where the natives went. If I were going to reject or be rejected, I wanted it to be with a different kind of person than those whom I rejected or who rejected me in Manhattan. That afternoon I practiced my Spanish. *Cómo se llama?*—What is your name?—though it is said in the third person, as if you were talking to someone about somebody else. *Quiere usted bailar?*—Do you want to dance?—a bit formal, but the book was clear about not using *tu* when you didn't know someone—even someone you might end up exchanging saliva with a couple hours later. The *usted* worried me; it had an ugly Germanic ring.

There was an outside bar at our guest house, where people would gather in the evening before going out to dinner. I sat there with a cuba libre, partly to kill time, partly to see what the women were wearing, partly because of my ineradicable hopes. A Puerto Rican man in his early forties sat down next to me; he was slightly overweight, but good-looking in the Latin way. After a few minutes of silence he asked me if I was having a good time.

"Not really," I said.

"No? I am always so happy here."

"Maybe if I knew somebody. I think I should have gone to someplace tiny, with hardly any people."

"I have just the spot for you," he said. "Vieques. I go there all the time—it's a little island off the coast. Twenty minutes on the airplane and you're there." I wrote the name of the island down, and the airline that flew there.

"The women here aren't very friendly," I said, glancing at the couples locked in their claustrophobic worlds. I expected him to be sympathetic, but he shrugged.

"What can you expect? They're on vacation. They come to this place because they know it's safe."

"I'm on vacation too," I protested. He bought me a drink. He told me he was married, but sometimes he came here to get away from his wife, who lived on the other side of the island. "Do you want to have dinner?" I asked him.

"I'm sorry, I'm meeting some friends." I hoped he would ask me to join them, but he didn't. No doubt they were men, going to some male place where they didn't want to be bothered with someone like me. I talked with him till he left to dress for dinner. The women drank their pre-dinner cocktails in their silk shirts and gold chains, white pants with pleats in them, makeup. What they wore was of no use to me; I had nothing like that in my hotel room, nor in my closet back home, nor would I have wanted to.

I decided to wear a pair of gold jeans a friend had stolen from a chic Italian boutique in New York; they were too tight for her and she had given them to me. If the label of this boutique had not been on the pants I could not have brought myself to wear them; they looked like they came from one of those cheap places that lined Union Square before it got cleaned up. "Puerto Rican stores," my mother used to call them, and though I had protested I had secretly felt that she was right. And yet, I had not seen anything remotely resembling gold jeans on anybody in San Juan. On the contrary, people here seemed to dress more formally and conservatively than in New York City. I told myself that was because I hadn't yet gone to the bars where women like me hung out. I told myself that in any case I didn't care what people thought, at least I would be noticed: I was tired of being invisible.

In my gold pants, before dusk, I walked towards town on the main road of the Condado. You would have thought I was leading a parade: almost every car that passed had to slow down and shout something out the window to me. *Hija de puta, puerca, vendámelos, prostituta!*—even women stopped to shout mean and half-intelligible things at me out the windows of their white convertibles. I was glad I didn't know Spanish better. My face burned but I refused to go back; I didn't like them any more than they liked me.

When I couldn't take it any more, I retreated into a

dark and empty restaurant, where I ate some mediocre *carne asada*. Now that the effect of the cuba libres had worn off I felt a bit depressed, and I ordered a double espresso to wake myself up. My bravado was gone and I wished I was back at the motel reading a book or lying on the sand. But if I began to pay attention to that coward's voice within I would never be able to do anything or go anywhere, so I forced myself to head for the disco. According to the map it was near the restaurant where I had eaten, but I was unable to find the street. I asked people directions but this was no help, either because my Spanish was bad or because people were deliberately misleading me on account of my gold pants.

After half an hour of fruitless wandering I hopped in a taxi. The man shook his head and refused to move. In the luxury of his being unable to understand me I told him in English that he was a closety faggot, that his wife was a whore, that I had fucked his daughter's brains out all last night. When I stopped screaming he got out of the cab and, motioning me to follow him, led me across the street and down a little alley. He stopped in front of a building. It was the place I was looking for. He refused my tip.

I walked up the stairs to the entrance to the disco. The man who took the money seemed worried I didn't know what kind of place it was and kept pointing to several men standing together by the door. "*Sí, sí, yo comprendo,*" I assured him, but he wouldn't take my money. Through the closed door I could hear the music. It was Latin rather than disco, but New York is in many ways a Latin city and I felt at home. Finally two women came up the stairs together; they were holding hands and when I didn't pass out from astonishment or shock, the man finally accepted my money and let me follow them in.

The front room was an old-fashioned bar with large "antiqued" mirrors and flocked red wallpaper and banquettes; it didn't exactly resemble any bar I had ever been in, and yet it felt familiar, like a dream of a bar. Beyond it was the dancing area, a huge room with a mirrored revolving ball that hung from the ceiling and reflected colored lights onto the floor, the walls, your eyes. It was not yet eleven, but the rooms were already crowded.

The biggest difference from what I was used to in New York was the clothing. Whereas on Christopher Street in the Village men walked around in jeans, plaid shirts, cowboy boots, and carefully trimmed three-day-old beards, here the iconography was more direct: close-fitting pants made at least partially of some synthetic material, pullover knit shirts in bright colors or dress shirts in stripes and patterns, clean-shaven faces with coconut-smelling pomade slicking down their hair, highly polished pointy shoes as contoured as their pants hugging their crotch.

But it was the women who were the real surprise. Either they wore high heels and fancy low-cut dresses that sharply outlined their bodies, huge amounts of dark mascara and bright red lipstick swabbed on their faces, or they had on dark blue or black suits, white shirts, and wingtip cordovan shoes, their faces plain and unmade-up, with short, slicked-back hair. Some looked like flowers and some looked like men, but either way they didn't look anything like me— or the blue-jeaned hippies, tweed-blazered businesswomen, or polyestered secretaries you saw in New York bars. I had seen women dressed like this before, back when we were just beginning to talk about ourselves with excitement, in bars where women who knew nothing of this talk still dressed in ways that were a sign of the past we were trying to destroy. In an odd and embarrassing fashion they had excited me, these women that bound their breasts to hide the fact that they were women, these women that would not let you touch them "down there" because they could not admit they were not men, and I had often wondered what it would be like to go home with one of them. But they were too butch for me to come on to them, and I was not femme enough for them to come on to me.

Everyone in the bar stared at me—perhaps it is more accurate to say they stared at my gold pants. Those who did not have the guts to stare at them directly were staring at them in the mirror, where, amidst the black and gray and brown pants, the brown legs with black stockings, shone two pillars of gold. Suddenly I remembered my bad luck with Latin women. In all the nights I had spent at bars I had never succeeded in persuading a *latina* to come home with me. The closest I had come was dancing for about an hour with a *puertorriqueña* at the Sahara. We kissed a little, then she asked me what I liked to do in bed. When I told her she said she was sorry, but I was not what she needed me to be.

I realized my eyes had focused on a woman in a dark blue dress with high black heels. She seemed to be looking at me too, with deep brown cow eyes like those of someone I used to love, though at the moment I could not remember who this was. It made me feel as if I knew her, so I got up the nerve to walk over to her.

"*Quiere usted bailar?*" I asked. She looked at me strangely. "*Quiere usted bailar?*"

"*No comprendo.*"

"*Quiere usted bailar.* You know, *dance*," I said in desperation, pointing to the dance floor. She walked away. I started to follow her, thinking she was leading me to the disco area, but she went over to some people she knew. She said something to them and they began giggling at me. I turned to my right. A woman stood near me; I didn't even know what she looked like. Who cared what she looked like if only she would help me get away from this spot? *"Quiere usted bailar?"* I asked.

"Quieres bailar?" she said back.

"Sí," I said, and began heading for the dance floor.

"No," she shook her head, then repeated: *"Quieres bailar?"*

"Sí. Quiero bailar." I took her hand, but she shook it off. I pointed to the couples dancing. Again she shook her head.

I was dying to leave, but I forced myself to go back to the bar and order a drink. A cuba libre—coke to keep me up, rum to calm me down, *libre* for all the faggots stuck in Castro's prisons, though I didn't know about this then. Perhaps, I should say, I didn't want to know about this then. I drank it quickly, with my eyes straight ahead, then I ordered another. So what if I got drunk? It would change the state of my mind, if not to something better, then to something different.

I tried to smile to show I was at ease, but of course it is difficult and unconvincing to do this when you know that the people who are looking at you know you have no reason to be so. In spite of my attempts to think ego-enhancing thoughts, all I could envision was the hideous walk down the Condado, the parade of epithets pouring out of cars. I remembered the vacation I had pictured: empty curved beaches surrounded by palms, women of various sexes all in love with me. What had been going through my head that of all the places in the world I ended up here? What was the matter with me that I unfailingly chose the wrong bar, the wrong clothing, the wrong person? Surely it couldn't be accident; either God had something in for me, or a perverse worm inside me was intent on compensating for an undeserved good fortune that years ago I had thought I had had.

"She was trying to tell you how you say," said a man's voice at my shoulder.

"What?"

"*Quieres bailar*. Do you want to dance."

"*Quieres bailar*," I repeated. "That's much prettier."

"*Usted* is formal."

"*Sí*, I know. But the *libro*—"

"*Quieres bailar?*" he said.

"*Yo comprendo*," I said. "*Quieres bailar*."

"No," he said. "Do you want to dance?"

I assumed it was pity. He was tall for a Puerto Rican, dark and somewhat younger than me. He wore a knit shirt and tan pants with a slim black belt and, like everybody on the dance floor except me, was a wonderful dancer. The music was disco now and we did the hustle, then it switched to a salsa beat. After each dance I stopped to give him a chance to move away, but despite my inadequacies he kept on dancing with me. No woman would be so kind.

I tried to imitate the movements of the people around me as they undulated to the music. After a while I began to sweat, and the heat and wetness aided my exertions. Or perhaps it wasn't that I was actually dancing so much better, but that my self-consciousness about how I was dancing began to disappear. The sexiness I secretly believed was always hidden within me began to rise to the surface, and I felt I could seduce my partner, or anyone—that it didn't depend on how I danced or looked but merely on how I felt about how I danced or looked. I told myself the stares I had been and was still receiving expressed not hostility, but admiration for my sexiness and guts. Women liked odd things, that was why heterosexual women fell into bed so easily with women like me; all you had to do was ask. Women who liked women were far more discriminating, but the women in this bar who were dressed like women resembled heterosexual women much more than they resembled gay women; in fact, they looked far more like heterosexual women than the heterosexual women I knew in New York.

The man I was dancing with told me his name was Juan, that he sold televisions in an appliance store, that he lived with an older man named Carlos who was in Mexico City for a week on business. Juan was not supposed to make love with anybody else, but perhaps he would tonight. If Carlos found out he would end the relationship. Spanish men—and women also—were incredibly jealous. Juan had broken off with his previous lover, whom he had lived with for four years, because he had found out that he was cheating on him with a woman. Juan had discovered this just before they were going on a vacation together, and as it was too late to cancel the reservations he had said nothing until they arrived back at the San Juan airport. As they were standing at the baggage pickup he told his lover he would never see him again.

"Was he gay or straight?" I asked.

"My lover." He almost spat. "He is a pig."

I wondered if I was supposed to sleep with Juan in return for his asking me to dance, in some kind of revenge for his ex-lover's betraying him with a woman.

At a lull in the music—that period every half hour when you're supposed to buy a beer—Juan excused himself to go to the bathroom.

I felt sweaty, hot, sexy. Again I saw the woman with the dark blue dress, the high heels, the cow eyes, staring at me.

Almost with a swagger I walked over to her.

"Quieres bailar?" I asked, with a slight Castilian lisp, holding out my hand.

She looked at me in disgust, then walked away, in a language anyone could understand.

Juan didn't return from the bathroom. The next day I went to the airport to fly to Vieques, but the pilot of my tiny plane told me the Navy was in the midst of its annual maneuvers there and I should go to Culebra instead. Culebra was like Vieques, only smaller. There was a guest house but it was expensive; if I wanted, I could stay with the pilot in the house the airline rented for him on Culebra, so that he could fly emergency flights to San Juan if anybody on the island got sick during the night. There was no hospital on Culebra.

Many interesting things happened to me on Culebra. I learned to scuba dive, I rode a pony bareback on the beach, I woke at dawn when the cocks began crowing, I watched white puffs from naval artillery rounds floating over the beaches of Vieques, I listened to "Rumours" by Fleetwood Mac—the pilot's favorite album—a minimum of three hours every day.

One night around eleven I sat in the co-pilot's seat next to him for twenty minutes as he took a girl who had a stomach ache and her family to San Juan (emergency flights were free so there was a tendency for people to get sick in the middle of the night). On the return flight he shut off all lights but those on the instrument panel and told me to take over the controls. There were lights in the sky above and lights from the sky reflected on the water below and there were lights on the island ahead, and though I thought I was keeping level he told me I was descending at two hundred feet a minute. Back home I let him put his hand in my vagina. There was already a tampax in there and when his hand pushed on it I got an orgasm. It was the first time I had gotten one that way. In the morning when he tried to do this again I told him no, it had been a one-time thing due partly to his astonishingly strong marijuana. The next afternoon he brought two young women—girls, really—back with him on the evening flight. They were blond and from Argentina and their fathers had big jobs in the government. When the pilot lit a joint they told him what a degenerate he was, he was lucky he was an American, in Argentina it was considered worse than murder. The pilot listened to this calmly, then passed me the joint. I didn't really feel like smoking, but to show them that I was lucky to be an American too, I took a few hits. I passed it to them and they took it—even though one of their fathers was big in the Security Police and had devised a way of taking care of people like us, they'd pour gasoline on the prisoners' mattresses and set them on fire and watch everybody burn to death. They giggled as they said this, perhaps because they thought they were funny, perhaps because they were smoking marijuana for the first time—at least they said it was the first time.

That night we went to the local island dance. There was no disco or Fleetwood Mac, the band used no electric or electronic instruments, the people scarcely moved their feet, yet it was the sexiest dancing I had ever seen in my life. The pilot, the scuba dive instructor, the two Argentinian girls, and I were the only nonnatives there, and though I felt conspicuous, it was in a different and better way than in the bar in San Juan. The pilot danced with one Argentinian girl and the scuba dive instructor danced with the other. I danced with several teenage boys who got a kick out of me, *la gringa*.

At a break in the music we went off into the bushes and smoked more of that astonishing marijuana. Roberta, the girl whose father was big in Security, began telling us more tales of torture and murder. The pilot and scuba dive instructor did not seem at all fazed by this, and as I got higher I began to wonder if maybe such things weren't weird at all, if maybe they were absolutely common, a state of affairs everyone knew about but me, that for all I knew existed in the United States, only I didn't know people important enough to tell me about it—or maybe even people had told me about it but I had pushed it out of my mind and was only now bothered about it because I was high and in some strange place where I felt more outside of things than usual. Did not horrible things happen every day on the streets of New York and did I not manage to ignore them?

I also realized men would do anything to get laid.

I walked over to where the teenage boys I had danced with were. But it was a teenage girl I faced as I asked, *"Quieres bailar?"*

She looked astonished, so I repeated the question.

"No comprendo," she said.

"Muy simple. Quiero bailar contigo. Quieres bailar conmigo?" The kids disappeared. Some older man came over and started shouting at me. I laughed, it was like an undubbed movie on the Spanish cable station in New York.

"Are you crazy?" the pilot ran over. He and Roberta dragged me away.

"Quieres bailar?" Isn't that right? What didn't she understand?"

"You want to get me thrown off the island?" asked the pilot.

"You know what we do to people like you back home?" asked Roberta. She had the same evil smile as when she had talked about the burning marijuana prisoners. I smiled back, then grabbed her head and stuck my tongue in her mouth.

"Quieres bailar?" I asked. The pilot laughed as I led her out onto the dance floor. She kept saying it was disgusting and I kept telling her she loved it, that everybody in the world was really gay and the point of marijuana was to enable people to admit this big secret. I also told her I knew she was just making up this stuff about her father, that deep down she was really the same as the pilot and me. I don't remember if I believed this as I was saying it.

The other girl had gone off with the scuba instructor, so by the end of the dance it was just the pilot, Roberta, and me. She pretended she was going to sleep alone, but the pilot and I joined her on her bed with a bottle of rum. Sometimes I passed out from the marijuana and the rum, and sometimes the pilot passed out, but Roberta was always there, ready in her strange way for whoever was awake. One time I woke up and saw her and the pilot in the moonlight. It was beautiful but very far away and I had a reluctance to interrupt them, the way I hate being interrupted during a movie. I fell asleep again, and when I woke up I found I was biting her breast. She screamed for the pilot to help, but he just sat smoking a joint.

"Mira," I said, sitting up on top of her. I took the joint out of the pilot's mouth and held it near her right breast. I began talking to her softly, mostly in English but using the few Spanish words I knew, telling her I was going to do to her what her *padre* did to the *maricones* and *mari-*

huanistas. As I talked I squeezed the nipple of her other breast, which got hard, then I leaned down and kissed her. Then I sat up and brought the hand with the joint next to her nipple.

She didn't move. "You don't have the guts," she said.

I lowered my hand. I *didn't* have the guts, but it was not so much the act I was scared of as the memories.

But my excitement was gone, and I let the pilot take over.

When the girl and her friend left the island the next day, they warned the pilot and the scuba dive instructor and me not to come to Argentina, because Roberta would tell her father all about us and he'd have us arrested and thrown into prison and we'd never get out. They were giggling when they said this. Then they took our photographs and gave us their addresses. The scuba instructor kissed his girl goodbye, while I got on the plane with the pilot to fly them to the mainland. We didn't give them our last names or addresses.

There were passengers with us on the way back too, so I didn't get a chance to take over the controls.

"Did you believe those stories?" I asked the pilot when we got back to the house.

"Did I believe what?" he asked. He popped open a beer and lit a joint, then we headed off to a dinner of some famous local fish we had expressly ordered the restaurant to catch for us that day.

Although I stayed on Culebra till I got my scuba certification, I never did manage to get one of the local *puertorriqueñas* to dance with me. I'm an outsider in their world, as they are in mine, as the Argentinian girls surely are in a country no longer run—if it ever was—by their fathers' friends. In New York I continued my quest, going to Latin bars in a man's suit and a pair of oxford shoes borrowed from a friend who likes to dress up. One night I finally succeeded, but it didn't mean what it should have, because I am who I am and not who I am not, and the girl I brought home quickly realized it.

iowa

Years ago, in the midwest, at one of the more prestigious writing schools, I had a crush on one of the students, a poet named Ellie who is now rather famous. But back then Ellie wasn't famous, she was a southern hick who had gone to her state university—the kind that's known more for its football teams than its poets. She was tall and thin and blond; the combination of her Alabamian decorousness, poetic sensitivity, and southern sluttishness drove me absolutely wild. Something about her implied she could fuck truck drivers as easily as poets and professors; I felt in competition with all the guys in town. We were friends, and as we walked by the river she'd talk about the guy she had slept with the previous night, or was thinking of sleeping with that night or the next, the ones who were great fucks and the ones I shouldn't go near. She knew who ejaculated prematurely, who ground his teeth in the night, who had the good dope, and who could make you laugh. To please her and to be able to talk with her about something other than poetry—about which I knew nothing—I diligently tried to fuck the same guys she did. She didn't care. This was the era of sharing, the same guys were slept with by all the girls we knew. Sometimes I'd think the real reason we did it was not the sex, but the conversation afterward—not with the guys but between ourselves.

Now that I think of it, perhaps that's why the men did it too, though at the time I thought they just wanted to get laid. This was a long time ago, when people still wanted to get laid.

Of course I may be misinterpreting all this; perhaps the impulses that brought men and women together were simple and sexual. Just because they weren't for me didn't mean they weren't for everybody else. I was trying to prove I was normal by sleeping with men the way other women did, although the more I did it the more unconvincing it became—not just to myself but probably to everybody else as well. It was unconvincing because my responses were off and it was impossible to hide this. I tried to disguise my lack of enthusiasm by an assumed enthusiasm that was totally false and which the men I was with must have known was false but which they pretended to believe as an excuse to continue doing things with me. If we had been honest, not only could I not have slept with them but they could not have slept with me.

Whatever my motives, it seemed the closest I could come to Ellie was in sleeping with the people who had slept with her. I wished these people had not been men, but they were men. If a man seemed to prefer me to Ellie I became disappointed in him; it showed he had bad taste.

Ellie and I were walking by the railroad tracks. It was one of those unexpectedly hot days that occur sometimes in spring. She carried a little pad and pen and I did too, though I was not in the habit of getting insights on walks. But I wanted to show her I was as sensitive and esthetic as she was, and occasionally I stopped to write things down. I would do anything to please her. I had begun reading poetry, I even tried (rather badly) to write it, I listened seriously to her opinions about novels—though theoretically I was the expert in that field. And all the time we were talking about literature, I was thinking about the glow the sun made around her face, about how much I loved her, and what she would say if I told her this.

My way of telling her this was to talk about my abnormal impulses, my desire to be normal, and how I couldn't talk about this to anybody because it was too disgusting.

"You're talking about it to me," she said.

"That's different. You're . . ."

"I'm what?"

"Well, a poet," I said lamely, though this had nothing to do with it.

I told her I knew that people who liked to do what I did were supposed to be sick, but I didn't feel sick, I just felt horny.

"This minute or in general?"

"In general *and* this minute." I stared at her a second, then looked at the ground, where two silver lines glared up at me. There was no danger, the trains didn't run anymore. This was so long ago, the trains hadn't been started up again to be stopped again. I squinted my eyes at the sun reflecting off the silver. I heard a buzzing: cicadas? crickets? bees? my blood pounding inside my head?

"What do you do about it?"

I wanted to show her what I did about it by turning into John Wayne and grabbing her, but it was broad daylight, the act was illegal and disgusting, she seemed to be flirting but surely if she were contemplating doing something so beyond the bounds of accepted behavior she wouldn't be smiling like that, she'd be feeling disgusted and nauseated and guilty as I had long ago, as I did even now much of the time. I wanted to ask her if she'd have sex with me but I was scared if I said anything she'd stop being my friend. If she stopped being my friend I'd never get a chance to ask her this question at a time that might be more propitious than this particular moment—say, when it was night and she was so tired and stoned she wouldn't know what she was doing.

"I don't know. What do *you* do about it?" I said lamely. She laughed and began singing a song about a guy who was going to be hanged for a crime he hadn't committed because his alibi was that he'd slept with his best friend's wife. It was a modern version of an old folk song that had recently been released by some country rock group. She had a high voice that quavered slightly and occasionally fell a little off-key. I sat down between the tracks on a piece of rotted wood and pulled out a stem of that long grass with teeny white flowers at the end of it and stuck it in my mouth. Did I forget to mention we were slightly stoned on the remnants of a joint she had in her pocket?

As I sat there listening to Ellie sing, I realized I was happy. Since then I have experienced moments of greater ecstasy but I don't think I was ever happier with a simple and pure kind of happiness than I was at that moment, and I wonder if I have ever been so again. Perhaps it was the simplicity of the times—me and the times. A revolution was about to occur in the country that would change everything in ways we weren't sure of but which would certainly eliminate war, imperialism, racism, and the taking of required courses in college. I didn't even consider the possibility that this revolution might make it okay for people like me to sleep with other people like me without being thought of as abnormal or sick; even if things like that had been able to be discussed I wouldn't have known who to discuss them with because people like us had not yet begun to talk about ourselves as a group; there weren't even any names for ourselves except the old, imperial, insulting ones. When I thought about my condition it was always as a condition, a sickness, an affliction that was not my fault but for which I was forever going to be blamed.

In a way I felt it was right for me to be blamed for this. Or perhaps, not exactly for this, but for something else for which I was responsible, and of which this was the clearest symptom. My mother called it my "coldness," but I think "coldness" was just another symptom of this thing and not the thing itself. I don't know how to express exactly what it was, but it involved some kind of refusal. A refusal to like milk, a refusal to go to bed on time, a refusal to pretend that there was anything sane and normal about a family.

In retrospect it seems impossible to believe I believed in the possibility—let alone the actuality—of there being a revolution that would change such things as war, racism, imperialism. I'm a skeptical, even cynical, person, and back then I was even more so. As I've grown up I've become more innocent. I think it was that so many of the people who were supposed to know about such things believed in these changes that I began to tell myself they were likely to occur, the odds had to be against so many intelligent people being wrong—the logic I now use when I hear about people who have seen ghosts or taken trips on saucer-shaped objects that fly.

I have never seen a ghost, and I am not willing to change my worldview to accommodate the existence of ghosts (I'm not even willing to change my worldview to accommodate the fact that the table my computer sits on isn't solid but merely a probability system of energy points), but I think it probable, in a statistical sense, that there are ghosts. Scientists have all sorts of "rational" explanations for the appearances of white-appareled apparitions, odd-shaped flying objects, and houses in which radios, plates, and chairs are dashed about against the walls, and I'm willing to concede that many—perhaps even most—of these events have unexciting interpretations. On the other hand, there need not be many ghost sightings for the existence of ghosts to be validated; one will suffice.

Sitting in between the railroad tracks as Ellie sang this new old song slightly off key, the sun making the surface of my closed eyelids a screen of orangey red, the lawn-mowed taste of a piece of fresh grass in my mouth, the buzzing of the cicadas in my ears, the touch of my shirt on my skin and the slight pressing of pebbles into my ass: can you blame me for not opening my mouth and reducing the possibilities of the moment to a single question?—though beneath all these other perceptions was a kind of buzzing that was like the buzzing of a certain kind of marijuana, except that I heard it sometimes with Ellie when I wasn't smoking marijuana, not just that afternoon but much of the time I was with her, and sometimes even when I was thinking about her when she wasn't actually there.

I felt she would be appalled if she knew this—justifiably

appalled. I was appalled, and it was under my control, insofar as love is within one's control.

I had had crushes before but I felt this was my first grown-up love.

"We'd better go back," she said.

I stood up. "Why?"

"I'm supposed to see *Yellow Submarine* with Cal."

"I thought you told me he fucks funny."

"Melodramatic maybe, rather than funny." We giggled.

There was a time when people took drugs not so they could stay awake for days trying to figure out ways to buy companies that did not need or want to be bought, or to prolong the period of time in which their penises could remain distended or their mouths continue talking, but to alter their perceptions of the world. Hallucinogens were supposed to accomplish in the mental sphere what the revolution was going to accomplish in the physical—only whereas the revolution was forever, a drug trip was only for a discrete period of time. But the forever never came, and now it is the drugs that are my most lasting memory of those days. Drugs and money. Things didn't cost anything then, you could stick out your thumb and live for free if you wanted; it took me years to realize this was no longer the case. Although I lived through this era and remember it clearly, it seems almost impossible that what I'm talking about really happened—though I also know, the way I know the dates of Waterloo and the Paris Commune, that everything I'm saying is true.

I have always been nervous about the relation of my mind to the rest of my body. I worry about breathing, I worry about what keeps a ring on my finger and a loafer on my foot, or what will happen if my body forgets for one subliminal instant to keep my sphincter muscle closed until I am sitting on a toilet. So you can imagine how I felt about placing in my mouth a blue-and-white pill that *Life* magazine assured you would make you see snakes. But there was another fear too, of being thought abnormal, of being conspicuous in the wrong sort of way, of not being part of the group that was the most important group in whatever situation I found myself in, and as this group was beginning to swallow these pills it became clear to me I had to do this too.

I told myself it wouldn't be so terrible if I went insane, that way maybe people would leave me alone and I could sleep with women. I would be so outside the pale of normalcy that nothing I could do would matter.

I told myself it wouldn't matter if I went insane because I was already insane. Only by constant and heroic efforts of will was I able to act normal enough to give the impression of sanity—if indeed I gave the impression of sanity. I felt the people around me were locked in a kind of pretense to pretend I was sane. Possibly this was because they liked me, but more likely it was out of politeness, because they were afraid that if they said anything it would throw me even farther over the edge.

I felt that people liked my insanity because it gave me freedom to say things that maybe other people wouldn't. But they were wrong. I said these things not out of my insanity but out of my hysteria that I was boring and had nothing to say. Some people, like Ellie, were able to be silent at a party and people would go over and talk to them anyway. But when I tried to imitate her, people would ask me what was the matter, why was I in such a bad mood?

I didn't resent Ellie for this at all. It merely confirmed me in my belief that she was a special human being worthy of my passion and attention.

I sat outside in the sun, a halo around my body, staring into Tony's eyes. Tony was the dog, and it seemed if only I thought hard enough, I would know what Tony was thinking. No, I *knew* what Tony was thinking; he was thinking about what I was thinking about, which was thinking about him.

I told Tony I loved him—not out of desire, as one did human beings—but with a pure and simple love born of the perfect understanding between us. There was a halo around him too.

In the midst of my recital he wandered away and began scratching in the dirt for a place in which to lay his shit. This seemed a physical equivalent of what human beings did in the mental sphere. But because it was physical it seemed more honest, and it made me wish I could be pure and simple like a dog, with no desires except what I was going to eat and where I was going to shit. To show Tony I understood him, even if in an imperfect human way, I lay on my stomach on the grass and began to dig my fingernails through the grass into the dirt. It felt cool and soft and good, though under my fingernails it looked like shit. I smelled it, in case I had stuck my fingers where Tony had buried his shit, but it smelled fine. I started to scrape the dirt out with a twig, then realized it looked rather pretty. Not pretty as in "pretty," but as in "interesting." As were my fingers—pink and brown and gray and white, with intersecting lines of varying depths and directions on the palm and around the joints, several minor blue bruises and one dark reddish-brown scab, a wart on the ring finger; then the hand itself: calluses on the palm, little hills on the back we called "knuckles," dunes and shadows and rivers of blue veins flowing through transparent skin that glowed red from my blood when you held it up to the sun. All this was very interesting—interesting and unexpected and it had nothing to do with snakes.

It had nothing to do with snakes. It had nothing to do with anything I knew. It was the first time in my life I had not known how things would be ahead of time and I began laughing hysterically at the thought that I could be surprised. I, *who knew everything*, could be surprised! And what I was doing was not just unimagined, but unimaginable; even if I had thought about it forever, I could not have figured it out. It was more surprising, even, than kissing a woman. Then I realized I hadn't thought of Ellie—even once—during the entire trip, though the point of the trip had been to impress her with my wild recklessness. I realized it was the longest period of time I had not thought of Ellie since meeting her.

But once I thought of her, I was unable to think of anything else. Perhaps I was less high, perhaps the pill had reached the space where I had stacked my emotions. She was in my mind, but not in my physical presence. This seemed a waste of the universe's resources. Why should I be thinking about someone who was not there when I could be thinking about someone who was there? I should think about something else, or I should be with Ellie.

I tried to concentrate on the present. I was next to a large round doughnut of black rubber that itself seemed a presence. A few feet away there was another one. I could see others too, underneath a huge shiny object that was holding these round black presences down. The shiny object was something like a gigantic vacuum cleaner, and something like a gigantic bug. When I reached out to touch it I felt an intense sensation at the end of my finger— either "hot" or "cold," though I wasn't sure which. The shiny object had a name too: "car." I remembered cars: I had driven out to John's farm in one that very day. If a car could drive me out to the farm, a car could drive me into town to see Ellie.

I stood up. I put my hand to the silver that reminded me of the railroad tracks where I had walked with Ellie and opened the door. I kept pushing on the gas pedal but the car didn't move. I couldn't figure out why. But it seemed a message: I was not to have what I wanted. This had happened before, all my life.

John walked over. It was his car. "What are you doing?" he asked. "It's got to be boiling in there." He opened the door and rolled down the window. I shut the door but left the window open and leaned out over it, my elbow on the burning metal. I felt like someone in a movie driving cross country. John looked quite pretty in the sun, and I felt, had I been someone else, I could have loved him.

"The car is broken," I said.

"You need a key."

I laughed hysterically. "A key!" The car needed a *key*; the *key* was the key to the mystery of why the car wouldn't run. For the first time I felt I really understood what a pun was. I tried to explain this to John, but he hadn't taken any pills, he was there to take care of us if something bad happened.

"I thought Ellie was going to be tripping with us," I said, when I had calmed down.

John shrugged. "She was supposed to be coming with Joan. I don't know what happened."

"Maybe she was late and wants to be here. We should get her. I'll go. You stay here and take care of everybody."

"It's too late," he said. "Everybody's already taken the pills."

"Ellie's hip. She can catch up. Don't you think she's hip?"

"Yeah. Sure." He glowed a coppery red; I knew he had slept with her last week. I also knew, whereas he didn't, that she wasn't planning to do it again.

"Give me the key," I said. "The car needs the key."

"You can't drive."

"I've slept with you," I giggled. "You should give me the key."

"I need the car in case somebody freaks out. You can call a taxi if you really want. But it costs a lot of money."

"I don't know why people won't do things when you really want them to," I said. And I didn't.

John walked away. I sat in the car. I knew there was a way to start the car that people used when they wanted to borrow cars that weren't theirs. I pushed pedals and rolled down windows and moved the lever on the wheel back and forth but nothing happened. The whole thing seemed ridiculously complicated. I stared at the narrow hole— *slit*—where the key had to be inserted to start the car in the simple, stupid way. I took a pen that was stuck in the crack between the bottom and the back of the passenger seat and tried to put it in the hole, but that didn't start the car either. Then it occurred to me that the whole point of the key was to limit access to the car so that only people who had the key could have use of the car. But this meant there were a lot more cars in the world than were necessary; the world would be a much better place if you could use whatever car was around when you needed it, and when you were done just leave it there for somebody else to use.

And suppose John lost the key? The key was a permission system for using the car, but why give power over your possessions to a piece of metal? It was hot in the car. The round silver hoop of the steering wheel burned into my hand. Normally I couldn't have stood it but I pretended I was in the desert and it was fine.

John came over again. He got inside with me. His sweat was beautiful, you could see colors in it like the rainbow. "It's really hot in here," he said.

"I like to be hot," I said.

"I think you should come out. I'm getting worried about you. Do you know how long you've been in this car?"

"I need to see Ellie," I said. The little voice in my head, the one that never shut up, the one that even now prevented me from having hallucinations like everybody else, told me this was a dangerous thing to say, but I couldn't help myself.

"Drop it," he said. "You'll get on a bummer."

"I'm not on a bummer. I'm happy. Very, very happy." I laughed so hard tears flowed out of my eyes. "But I need to talk about it."

"I'll talk about it if you get out of the car."

I had never been able to talk about Ellie to anybody before so I got out of the car, though I sat down right next to the open door in case John changed his mind about giving me the key or driving me to Ellie's. Only when I was outside in the cooler air did I realize how hot it had been in the car. I lay down in the grass. It tickled my nose. From my vantage point on the ground the pieces of grass looked very large, giant fronds taller than I was. An ant began to crawl up my arm. I let him; he was a being with desires like me. He wore a coat of many colors: red, black, brown, a hint of green and blue, a little yellow. Usually I did not pay attention and saw only the black coat. He was large too, a gigantic creature as tall as my eye, though my arm was even more monstrous—a huge bridge he was trying to crawl over.

Ellie was a bridge too; she stood between me and happiness, or ecstasy, or peace.

I told John my sanity lay in Ellie's hands. I told him that if I had been thinking about a Coca-Cola for hours he would get it for me without thinking, if he were even the slightest bit a decent human being. He would get it for me even if he weren't a decent human being, but just because he had slept with me.

"Do you want a Coke?" he asked.

"That's not what I meant."

"Anyway, do you want a Coke?"

Actually, it sounded pretty good, its coldness and its sweetness. But there was also a kind of dryness behind the sweetness, and I might choke and drown swallowing it. "I don't know," I said.

"I'll get you one. You must be pretty thirsty."

He was a kaleidoscope as he walked across the lawn. I had totally forgotten about him by the time he came back.

"Is this a Coke?" I asked him. "It looks funny."

"It's Dr. Pepper."

"Oh." I wetted my lips with it. "It's very good," I said. "In certain ways I think it's even better." I paused. "But maybe not the most important ways," I giggled.

I asked him what was the difference between him getting me a Coke if I wanted one and him not getting me Ellie, if I wanted her.

"I've slept with Ellie, you know," he said.

"I know." I began to explain to him the absurdity of my being here and her being there, but metaphysics entered the picture ("What did it mean to be 'here,' if she was in my head, and where was 'here'?" and so on), then epistemology ("How did I know I wanted her to be here; just because a picture of a person was in my head, did this mean I wanted to be with them?" etc.). The discussion was incredibly interesting, and I kept telling myself to remember things so I could write them down later. Once I even started for the house to get a pen, but I sort of got distracted along the way. Then I felt strange. I went over to the car and looked at my face in the rear-view mirror by the driver's door. With its blotches, pimples, lines, discolorations, bumps, and hairs, it was revolting. I lay down again on the grass. An ant crawled on my arm. His coat was black. I was down.

I was in Ellie's apartment. I had brought some pills for us to take, pills we would take together so that for once what was in my mind would also be in my physical presence. We were supposed to have taken the pills together and alone but other people had heard about the plan and decided to join us. Ellie had asked me if this was okay, and although it wasn't, of course I said yes. I had learned when I was very young how dangerous it was to be honest in your opinions; also I was scared if I told Ellie I wanted to be alone with her when we took the pills she would have figured out what was going through my head and said no.

Before swallowing the pills, we were supposed to drive out to John's farm, but in those days people were very loose about time, and by the time the last ones arrived the rest of us had already taken the pills and it was too late to start worrying about cars. I had wanted to recreate the circumstances of the previous trip at the farm, only with Ellie physically present instead of present only in my mind, and I felt my failure to do this was emblematic of something—something that I always felt had or had not happened in my life and which it was too late ever to go back and fix up. I also knew that the real problem wasn't that "it" was "too late," but that I continued to describe it to myself as such.

During the trip many things were on my mind: the skin on my face (glowing), the movement of my body through the air (no resistance), a buzz I felt would keep me forever in the present if I could only learn to replicate it. Almost never was I in the present and this was what I liked most about the drug; the world became so interesting in a visual, aural, sensory, and mental way that one's mind was totally occupied. I realized it was not the content of one's thoughts that was important, but their continuing progression through one's mind. When the experience was good it was interesting in a positive way and I liked my face, and when it was bad it was interesting in a negative way and I saw the skull beneath my bones, but at least it was interesting. And "it" was everything—the sun, the air, me, even other people. I felt I loved them totally and wanted never to be separated from them. I felt I was with a group of people who had shared a communion that would bind us to each other forever. I realized that liking was a question not of shared opinions but shared experiences. I realized Ellie's cat Rufus was as intelligent as me. (I'm not sure whether I realized the man who picked up the garbage was as intelligent as me.) I realized that if you looked closely the walls breathed. Sometimes I had trouble breathing but the way I convinced myself this was not a problem was not really any different than it was at other times; the fear may have been more intense, but then, I had greater strength to deal with it.

I kept trying to be in the same room as Ellie, but there was some speed in the pill we were taking that made her keep moving around. All I wanted was to be alone with her, but I always seemed to be entering the room either when someone else was there or else when she was about to leave, when it was too late. Then the drug got to be its strongest and I no longer had any self-consciousness about following her—but on the other hand it didn't seem so important. I was living completely in the present and if she was there that was wonderful and mind-occupying, but if she wasn't, my mind was equally occupied. So I wasn't really looking for her, it was the speed in the drug that propelled me into her bedroom—speed and a search for sunlight, for she had the corner room.

She was alone, sitting on the bed, her head against the backboard, flipping through a book.

"You're able to read?" I asked, astonished.

"In a way."

"What way?"

"Well," she said. "Very, very slowly."

We laughed a long time. "You have beautiful teeth," I said. I moved over to look more closely at them. They were not Jewish teeth like mine—yellow and chipped and lined up every which way—but the very essence of her southern, Protestant being: white as a toothpaste ad, with no patches of gray or brown, though occasionally she did smoke. "Would you mind opening your mouth?" I asked. She laughed but obliged me. I peered in. No silver either. "You don't get cavities?"

"No." I was so close I could have kissed her. I think maybe she expected me to kiss her, and that was why she had opened her mouth. It was fairly late in the afternoon and the sun slanted through the window across the room, falling on her bed, a book, a glass of water that made a little rainbow on the old wooden bureau she had gotten from Goodwill. The glass of water was very still, and tiny little bubbles—air pockets—were in it. It seemed to me if you put your head in the glass you could breathe those bubbles. The sun threw a bar of orange across her book, and her hand, and her face. It seemed very poignant, the only way someone with skin like hers could get a tan. Her hair had matted a little from sweat. She looked more beautiful than ever now that she was a little worn—or perhaps it was that I could connect with her beauty better now that it was worn. I had empathy; I knew what it was to be sweaty and tired and seeing things, I was just like her.

"Sometimes I feel like a dog around you," I said.

She laughed. "You mean now?"

"No. If I were a dog I—"

"What?"

I wanted to tell her that if I were a dog, I couldn't kiss her, but now I could kiss her. I knew absolutely that in this sunlight and in this room at this very moment I could kiss her, and she would kiss me back, and I could have everything I ever wanted. Do you realize what it means to a person like me who has never had anything they ever wanted to know they can have everything they've ever wanted? I looked at the sun and I looked at her hands and I looked at her teeth, in a mouth that was smiling at me.

I could have everything I ever wanted, but I held back. Now that I could have it, there was no need to rush the moment. Once I had it, it would change, and I would never have this moment—the moment of changing from not having to having—again. "Wait," I told myself. "You have all the time in the world." We were in it for the duration, and each minute was so long I could not even imagine the end. Every second was in itself complete and fulfilling and totally interesting. It was the best few minutes of my life, and if I could have stopped time there altogether I would have, and you would see me still in that room, the orange light hitting the dust beams in the air, and the water, and her southern smile.

Then someone walked in, and I listened to them talk as I looked at the sunlight careening around the room, and it was all right, and other people came in and joined us, and that was all right too, they were like cicadas, the hum of a lawn mower, the residual noise of the birth of the universe, a hum that was always there beneath life and yet was also part of life. My love was not separate and private, it was as much a part of the world as ferns or fish or dogs or air bubbles in water.

I looked out the window to the house across the street. The sun was now behind it and threw a huge shadow across the lawn. In a little while, as it went down further, the shadow would be in this room.

I looked at Ellie. If I couldn't be alone with her this instant, it would be too late.

Even as I thought it I knew it would not matter if I were alone with her in the room, it was already too late. It would not have occurred to me it would be too late unless it was already too late. The effects of the pill were still in my system and I was still high, but I was a little less high than I had been a few minutes before, and the difference was sufficient to have taken away just enough of my conviction in regard to kissing her to make it impossible to do this in a way that would make it impossible for her to refuse me—which was the only way I felt she would acquiesce.

I was not a man, and not being a man I had to be perfect.

I told myself I should do it now—in front of everybody—before my conviction disappeared even further.

I got up to do it, but even as I moved towards her the conviction lessened even more, so that I only picked up the glass of water. It was no longer a prism, just a glass of water.

She was no longer perfect either.

There were other trips, but because I was so intent on finding the perfect moment, I was less able to be in the absolute present than the people around me, and my consciousness of this created a distance between me and those around me so that I was never again able to be with Ellie with the perfect conviction that if I reached out my tongue to touch her mouth I would not be a dog in her eyes but a human being. I knew the self-consciousness was in myself and not the world and I tried all sorts of methods of getting rid of it: I talked about it, I was silent, I got stoned, I got drunk, I wrote down whatever I was feeling, and I made my mind a total blank. These efforts and my talking about how I was caught in my self-consciousness caused people to tell me that I was becoming a bummer and they no longer wanted to take pills with me. I promised to change, to shut up, to become a different person. I was sincere but of course I could not shut up, I could not become a different person.

Ellie remained my friend. She continued to tell me about the guys she slept with and the guys she didn't— John, for instance, who was really hung up on her—and I continued to tell her about the guys I slept with—John, for instance. I continued to have hopes, however, that the perfect moment would again arise. She had not fallen in love, she didn't sleep with any particular person more than a few times, and in a sense, though I knew I didn't have all the time in the world, I had time.

I told myself when I was alone that the real problem was that I was interested in Ellie, whereas she did not want someone to be interested in her, she wanted someone she could be interested in herself. I tried various ways to make myself more interesting to her—by talking more and more about my weirdness, even about how I was using my weirdness to make myself more interesting to her—but the more I talked, the more I could see interest in me draining from her eyes. I think the problem was that, despite my apparent narcissism, I was not really interested in myself. Rather, I was interested in myself in the presence of certain people—people who were interested in me rather than themselves when they were in my presence—but I could not be interested in myself in the presence of Ellie.

If I could not be interested in myself in the presence of Ellie, why should she be interested in me?

I knew she was not all that interesting, yet I was interested in her.

"Guess what?" she said to me one day. It was a dreary November afternoon, and we were sitting by the window in the Student Union before going to class. Sleet was falling in the river, and because I was alone with her I told myself I was happy—not as happy as I had been in the spring or summer, but still happy.

"What?" I asked. I had finished my coffee and was playing with my empty water glass, trying to balance the bottom edge in some sugar I had poured on the table. It was white and crystalline like the snow that was supposed to fall that night, and I told myself that once the whiteness came and everything was pure and the sun bounced off the snow and glared into my eyes the way it had in the summer everything would be all right again.

"I've fallen in love."

She looked at me. I told myself not to do something stupid. "Congratulations," I said dully.

"I realized something," she said. "I've never really been in love before."

"Really?" My voice was squeaking. I reached for her water. Air bubbles were in the glass, but I did not even imagine I could put my head in it and breathe them.

"I thought I'd been, but I wasn't. This is different."

I looked at her. I didn't know what to say. This time it really was too late. I told myself it had always been too late, it had been too late when I was born. Somehow this made me not responsible, and it freed me to say what I had been unable to say over those long summer days.

"I'm in love with you," I said. There was a long pause while she picked her bread and rolled it into little white balls. People still ate white bread then. "You don't seem surprised."

"I thought maybe you were," she said.

Tears began to run down my face. Despite my misery, I made sure to turn my face to the window so nobody could see them.

"I'm sorry."

"Me too," I said dumbly. I felt terrible, but I also felt a sick kind of relief.

We were silent a while. "You know, I wanted to sleep with you," she said finally.

"When?"

"Last summer. Like that day we were tripping."

"So why didn't you?" Somewhere during the conversation I had begun playing with my glass again, and I noticed now that I had finally got it balanced.

"I kept waiting," she said. "All you had to do was ask."

ibiza

I couldn't find a room in the main town on the island, which is also called Ibiza, so I had gone over to San Antonio, where the Germans and a few English were. Germans vacation differently than Americans; they often start out alone but they find other Germans, they go out for dinner in groups, nobody gets left out. The English drink lots of beer and beach their white fat bodies in the sun. They don't get tan, only red; you can hear their hideous accents miles away. There were no Americans but it didn't matter; they travel in twos or fours and stick to themselves, the quieter the place the better. Maybe it's because we don't know foreign languages and even when we do we don't know how to make conversation. The Spanish are elegant and disgusted by both Germans and English, though they like the French and Italians, even the Americans—probably because we're better-looking than the English and Germans. But the truth is, even when Germans are good-looking nobody likes them.

To get away from the Germans, I ended up spending much of my time in the town of Ibiza anyway. The gay bar was there, and most of the stuff worth seeing. It was past the famous period, but there were still plenty of hippie drop-outs, writing a little here and there, painting a bit, making jewelry, living on their incomes, selling drugs. The Americans had gone home, so these were mainly Europeans. I was sitting in a café near the bay when a beautiful girl of about seventeen walked over to my table and put one of those little embroidered wool shoulder bags down on the seat across from me. She was blond and thin and almost too young—even back then—for me. But I couldn't really believe she was after my body.

"You don't mind if I join you, do you?" she asked, first in Spanish, then in French.

"*Ah-wee.*" I tried to pronounce it like the French. "*Ça va bien.*"

"Oh, you're American."

"*Sí.* I mean *oui.*"

"I like Americans very much. They are so generous."

"Would you like something to drink?"

"Maybe a little Coca-Cola. It is so very hot," she looked up at the sky apologetically. I noticed her staring at my *jamón serrano*, and gave her half the sandwich. "Thank you," she said. "Perhaps I am a little hungry." She gobbled the food so I asked the waiter to bring us another sandwich.

"Are you staying in Ibiza?" I asked.

"Yes. Aren't you?"

"No. I got stuck in San Antonio. I couldn't find a place in town."

"That's too bad. I wanted to take a shower." She seemed to lose a little interest in me.

"Your shower is broken?"

"Not exactly."

"Where are you staying?"

"Here and there. With different people."

"Friends?"

"Friends. People I meet."

"Oh." Maybe she did want to spend the night with me.

"If you want, I can ask them if they know of a place here where you can stay," she offered.

"That would be great. I'm sick of the Germans."

She took lipstick out of her little bag, and applied it expertly without looking.

"I'll go now," she said, suddenly standing up.

"I could come with you," I said. "Are they near here?"

"It will be just a few moments. You will not have time to blink your eyes."

I did not expect to see her again, but it was very hot, so I was content to sit in the shade and read my book. I was reading stories set in hot and distant places, places like where I was or even more so. I felt like a character in a story, and was almost glad to have wasted my money on her lunch. I gazed at the handsome Spaniards around me in their bright shirts. They looked extraordinarily happy. Franco had recently died, and the entire country seemed to be on holiday.

When she came back I was so engrossed in my book I didn't notice her until I heard her plunk her bag down on the table. "They are not there, but why don't you meet us at the disco tonight?" She gave me directions how to get there.

"What time?"

"Not too late. About one, one-thirty."

"If you want, you can come to San Antonio to take a shower."

"That's a little far to go for a shower, isn't it?" she asked.

I went inside to pay the check. She started talking to the bartender. As soon as the owner went into the kitchen the bartender brought out a huge straw bag which he placed on top of the counter. She took some stuff from her little bag and put it in the big bag, then she took some stuff from the big bag and put it in the little bag. I looked inside the big bag. In it were several pairs of shoes, pants, shirts, a sweater, a makeup case, some underwear—less than I took when I went away for the weekend. "This is where you keep your clothing?" I asked.

"Yes."

"How long have you been here?"

"Four months. Maybe five."

She glanced around the bar, then quickly slipped off her T-shirt and put on a blouse. She was not wearing a bra. There were only a few people in the bar, and none of them seemed to notice this.

The disco was astonishing, a beautiful place with little bridges over water, flowers everywhere. I arrived about one, but it was quite empty. All the drinks were six dollars, even the Cokes. This was ten years ago. A half hour later people began to arrive. You could see from their tans and their clothing and the way they knew each other that they were mostly locals, not tourists. The men looked dazzling in their splendid patterned shirts and the women—in loose but sexy white dresses of coarse island cotton with flat sandals, or tight little skirts with heels—looked even better.

At two-thirty I started to leave. But just as I got outside I ran into the girl I had met that afternoon. "Are you going already?" she asked. "We are only now arriving."

Her friends were a motley crew: a man in his sixties, several boys in their late teens, a few women in their twenties and thirties. The men seemed as if they would be interested in men but it's hard to be sure about things like this in a foreign country, the clues are so different. I did not have on the right clothes and they looked me over without interest. I didn't even bother to ask them about the room. "Would you like a drink?" I asked the girl.

"They are very expensive."

"Yes. But that doesn't matter."

"I don't like alcohol. Maybe you would like to smoke?"

We left the disco and went behind the parking lot.

"Hash," I said. "How great. This is so hard to get in America."

"Really?"

"Yes. All we have is marijuana."

"How lucky you are," she said. "I love marijuana, and I'm not, what you say, so 'crazy' about hash."

"You should live in America, and I should live in Spain," I joked.

"I would like to visit America," she said seriously. "But I have no desire to live there."

I could not blame her. I was in a disco more beautiful and stylish than any I had seen in America, and this was true of the men and women in it too. It was past three, but the place was jammed. From what I could tell, the entire country was in *festivo*—not a fake *festivo*, like we had in America to celebrate things we no longer cared about, but a real one.

"How late does the disco stay open?" I asked.

She shrugged. "Six, seven o'clock. Until the people go

home. Nine in the morning, sometimes, if they're still dancing."

By four I could barely keep my eyes open. I asked the girl if she needed a place to spend the night.

"Oh no, I'm not like that," she said. "Anita! Anita!" She ran over to someone a little older than she was and embraced her. I assumed it was an excuse for getting away from me, but she turned around impatiently and motioned me to join them. "This is Anita. Anita, this is my friend from America. Have you seen Roberto? He owes me some money." She darted into the crowd.

"You're the one who's staying in San Antonio?" Anita asked me.

"Yes. With the Germans." I couldn't believe the girl had told anyone about me. If she had, had it been for a purpose? I looked at Anita more closely. She wasn't especially my type, but I had already spent several fruitless nights at the gay bar. "Where are you staying?"

"Oh, you know. Here and there."

"Maybe you would like to take a shower?" I asked.

"Maybe." She smiled.

Anita and I began spending our nights together. I was not particularly attracted to her, but I had been traveling for several months and it was good to rest and have someone to sleep with at night. Sometimes we had dinner, but we didn't have much to say to each other, so usually we just met in the evenings at some café in San Antonio. We'd take a walk by the water and then head to my hotel. I'd go upstairs first and she'd follow me a few minutes later, so I wouldn't have to pay the double rate for the room. She'd slip out in the morning before me, though on occasion she waited for me at the café so I could buy her coffee before she left to spend the day with her friends.

Once Anita brought Luisa, the friend who had introduced us, to the hotel so she could take a bath. Perhaps Luisa's luck in the main town was running out. I told Luisa she could use my room whenever she wanted, even when Anita wasn't with her. Once or twice she did this, though generally the two girls came together. Their toilette would usually take at least several hours, because it was not just a shower or bath but also finger- and toenail cutting and polishing, maybe a bit of a haircut. Or they would wash their clothes and drape them over the railing on my little balcony to dry. Sometimes they massaged each other and I wondered if they slept together when the tourists weren't around. I loved listening to them gossip in Spanish, even though I couldn't understand them. But I recognized a few odd words here and there, mostly adjectives and names of people and beaches. Sometimes I asked them what they were talking about, and they would revert to English for a while. It was always about the people they knew: who was sleeping with whom and where, which rich person could be counted on to take you out to dinner without fuss and which one couldn't. It confused me that Anita didn't pester me to take her out to dinner more, considering that obtaining a free meal was second in importance only to finding someplace to spend the night. I couldn't tell whether or not I should be flattered by the fact she continued to sleep with me even though in some sense I felt I wasn't very interesting to her.

Nor was our sex particularly good. She accused me of being too passive. I didn't like her enough to touch her very much, and I guess in some way I felt that my supplying the room should in some sense compensate for my lack of activity in bed. It disturbed me a little to be thinking the way men do, but perhaps not enough.

"It is Luisa you like best," she said one night. We had started to have sex but stopped in the middle. The kind of hotel I was in didn't have air-conditioning, and I was bothered by the wetness—the sweat of her body and the gunk on my hand.

I debated whether to be honest. "Well," I admitted. "She's more my type. I like blondes very much."

"It's not her real color," said Anita. "She bleaches it. Her real hair is dark, darker than mine."

This was impossible to believe. Luisa had taken enough showers in my bathroom for me to observe her hair and the way she treated it in great detail. She didn't bleach her hair and the roots weren't black. "You mean, bleaches it in the sun," I said.

"No. With peroxide. Always men are fooled by her," she said with some bitterness.

"You're not jealous?" I asked.

"Oh no. I just thought you should know this."

The next time I was alone with Luisa I told her that Anita said she bleached her hair. She laughed. I asked her if her hair was really black.

"Does it matter?" she asked.

"Well . . ."

"I will tell you what you want to hear," she said. "Do you prefer I bleach it or not?"

"I prefer you don't bleach it," I said.

"Good. Because I don't bleach it. Anita's an idiot."

"She sounded like she was jealous," I said. "But I know she can't be."

"Why not?"

"Because she doesn't like me very much."

"Why do you say that?"

"Oh. You know. For one thing, she doesn't do very much to me in bed."

"Do you do very much to her?" Luisa asked.

"Well . . . not exactly."

"Maybe you think because it is your hotel room you don't have to touch her?" She said this without rancor as she studied her hair in the mirror.

"Of course not."

I watched her do her hair. She was trying to put it up in different ways. She was having dinner that night with a wealthy man she had met several days ago. He was in his forties and she had not yet slept with him. She told me she wouldn't sleep with him unless he let her stay in his house for the rest of the summer—even when he was away. She had gotten a little tired of moving around.

"Actually, it's you I'm really attracted to," I admitted.

"Poor Anita. It's always that way. No wonder she hates me."

"She doesn't hate you," I said.

"Oh yes she does. I don't blame her really."

A few strands were loose at the back of her neck. They blew a little in the late afternoon breeze.

"Will you sleep with me?" I asked.

"I told you I'm not that way."

"How could I be worse than that fifty-year-old guy? I'll pay you a little something," I said. "I know you need the money."

"Anita will be angry."

"She won't. Anyway, we don't have to tell her."

"I have to," Luisa said. "She's my best friend."

"Not if it will hurt her." I walked behind Luisa, and bent down and kissed the back of her neck.

She turned around to face me. "All right," she said. "But only if you promise never to tell her."

"Of course. How much shall I give you?"

"Will ten American dollars be all right?"

"Yes." These were worth much more than they are now, especially in Spain.

She walked over to the bed and took off her shirt. "We mustn't take too long," she said, "or I'll be late for dinner."

The stuff we did and the way it was done was pretty similar to what happened between Anita and me, but I enjoyed it much more because I was so attracted to Luisa. She acted like she was enjoying it too, though of course I couldn't be sure. Right in the middle she got up to go to the bathroom. Frustrated, I listened to the toilet flush and waited for the light to shut off under the door. Then I heard her shout, "What time is it?" from the *baño*, and I knew the sex was over.

"Ocho menos cinco."

"Oh!" I heard the water come on.

I considered it bad taste to use my vibrator in the presence of other human beings, so I followed her into the bathroom and sat on the edge of the tub while she washed. "That wasn't too bad, was it?" I asked. I tried to put her hand between my legs, but she pulled it away.

"No. But you must realize, this was a once-in-a-time thing."

"Oh." Of course I had hoped she would fall in love with me. "At least it didn't disgust you, did it?"

"If it was going to disgust me I wouldn't have agreed to do it."

"But you couldn't have known what it was going to be like," I said.

"Why not?"

"You've never slept with a woman before."

"Are you crazy? It's Anita who hasn't slept with a woman before."

"What!" I thought of the casual—no, lackadaisical—way she had agreed to come home with me that first night. "I don't believe it."

"I knew in her heart she was that way, so I—what is the expression—'setted you up' with her. It would be better if you were nicer to her," she added.

"She doesn't like me," I said.

"That's not true. She likes you very much."

"I don't think so," I said. "I think you don't like me either, that you're just friends with me because of my hotel room."

"You're wrong. We both like you very much. What is the matter with you, that you are always thinking people don't like you?"

"I don't know."

While Luisa was putting on her makeup there was a knock on the door. It was Anita. She looked at the messed-up bed, and though there was no reason either Luisa or I couldn't have taken a nap, she knew instantly what had taken place and began screaming at Luisa in Spanish. Luisa sat there calmly, still fixing her hair, though every once in a while she tried to put in a word. When her hair was done, she stood up.

"I'm leaving," she said. "Anita, there is no need to be so upset. I have promise you this will not happen again."

"Oh yes. I should believe the words of the daughter of a whore!"

■ ■ ■

After Luisa left, Anita began sobbing. "How could you do this to me?" she kept repeating.

"I told you I was attracted to her," I said. The degree of her upset was surprising, and interesting—perhaps the most interesting thing I had noticed so far about her.

"Why? Just because of her phony hair. That is so silly, when she is such a horrible person."

"She introduced us," I said. "And in many ways she is a very good friend."

"Good friends don't betray you," she said. "I suppose now you will want to sleep with her instead of me."

"I want to sleep with you too," I said, though at the moment I couldn't have cared less.

"She won't sleep with you again. She always does this to people. How much did you make you pay her?" I thought of lying. "Don't lie, because she will tell me the truth—not because she is honest, but just to torture me." I tried not to laugh at the melodrama of her language.

"Ten dollars," I admitted.

"Then you must give me eleven dollars," she said.

"No."

"Why not?"

I told the easy part of the truth. "Because you've been doing it for free."

"No más," she said. "And you must also buy me dinner."

"No."

"Yes."

"No."

"Why not?"

Usually I would have lied, but I was tired and relaxed. "To be honest," I said. "It's not worth it to me."

We stared at each other. She slapped my face. I could hardly blame her. She pulled back her arm as if to do it again, but I grabbed her hand. Our faces were close to each other, and so I kissed her, for the first time with passion. Then we began clawing at each other.

"Luisa was right. You do like me," I said, several hours later. The bed was wet with sweat and other body fluids, but for once I didn't mind it. I felt almost tender toward her.

"Idiot. It was because you smelled like Luisa."

"You're in love with her?" I asked. Once I heard my astonished voice, I couldn't believe I hadn't figured this out before.

"Isn't everyone?" she said, rather bitterly.

a night on the town

For many years I did not believe in happiness, I did not believe in the possibility of change, I saw nothing but dullness stretching out in front of me. I wanted to become a spy, to give that dullness a hidden meaning no one would know but me, but my beliefs got in the way—my beliefs, and pieces of paper I had signed in favor of or against various causes and persons. So I lived the double life the only way available to me: after my regular evening with my regular friends, when dinner or the movies or the party or opening was over and the normals headed for home, I'd go to the bar instead.

Often the bar was boring, but it was not normal, which in itself made it interesting. The atmosphere was conducive to thought, and the thoughts weren't normal, so the experience acquired a richness. Often I told myself to remember my thoughts, and I would try to memorize them, forming a word with the initial letters of the thoughts which I would use to recall them later at home. For instance, CLSM (pronounced in my head as "clism"): "Coming out as erotic experience—Loneliness of God—S/M not sex, but to get to same *place* as sex." Sometimes my thoughts were so complicated or I was so drunk I would know this was impossible and I'd ask the bartender for a napkin. But more often than not the blue ink of the Flair pen would turn into lines of fur on the napkin, or the counter would be so wet from a beer or a wiped bar top that the paper itself would dissolve. Even the sweat from my hand as I clutched the napkin could destroy the words that were more memory systems for thoughts than thoughts themselves.

The next day, after usually vain attempts to transcribe the profound musings of the night before on my typewriter, I'd stuff the napkin in my desk, saving it for a day when my brain might work better. On acid you remember mostly other acid trips. I felt that if I could become high in exactly the same way and degree as I had been when I wrote the words down in the bar, I would remember what they meant.

Even when the letters did not dissolve, they were nonetheless often indecipherable, because of the terrible and illegible handwriting I had developed in childhood so that my mother could not read what I wrote and realize that she had given birth to someone who wasn't normal like her. Once I was no longer living with my mother this illegibility was a hindrance, but as much as I ordered myself to write slowly and carefully with big round letters, this was impossible; as soon as I got caught up in a thought (which was necessary for writing it down) I forgot my resolution, and my letters would revert to their original cramped and hasty forms.

I did not always go to the bar to pick someone up. Sometimes I was interested merely in listening to what people said, not only to me but to each other. I wanted to learn something about life, partly for the sake of knowledge, and partly so I would know better how to behave in places like this. I believed there were magic words which if I only knew them would enable me to go home with anyone I chose. Usually I believed these magic words weren't uttered with the mouth but with the body, which is why I spent so much time figuring out what to wear and how to stand, but sometimes I felt that words alone could do the trick. Deep down I knew that neither of these things was true, that it was partially a matter of words and body, but more than that a question of how these two went together, and even more than that a question of fate.

I detested fate. It was a sign that things were beyond my grasp.

I had been brought up to believe that if you tried very hard, all the good things you deserved would be coming to you. Examples from my life and history were clear evidence this wasn't true, yet I felt I could not give up this idea until my parents admitted it wasn't true. Until they did this, I would somehow remain in thrall to these beliefs.

The bar brought home to me these fallacies with peculiar force. I was surely the smartest person in the bar. No doubt I was the best writer in the bar. I may even have been the most famous person in the bar. Deep down I felt that in some way I was the best-looking person in the bar, though I would have had a hard time explaining to anybody else in precisely what way this was true. I think it was that in the faces or bodies of even the most attractive people in the bar I nearly always found something to disgust me, whereas I was used to my own disgusting things and they didn't bother me so very much. I suppose this is true for everyone, which is why people in the privacy of their apartments do things like pick their nose or flake dried skin off the bottom of their feet.

And yet, in spite of the obvious superiority of all aspects of my being, in the bar I was treated just like an ordinary person. This irritated and mystified and in an odd way intrigued me—and was perhaps the main reason I kept coming back to the bar.

A woman dressed in expensive bad taste walked over and began talking to me about my friend Brett. Rings and hoops dangled from her arms and ears. Neither her face nor her Brooklyn accent was familiar, and I assumed she was drunk. On the other hand, Brett's tastes were decidedly tacky. "You don't remember me, do you?" she asked.

"No," I admitted.

"We spent the night together once," she said. "I had blond hair then, maybe that's why you don't remember."

"I don't think so," I said. She wasn't at all my type.

"We did," she insisted. "The night of the big masquerade ball. When Katherine got drunk and got into a fight with Brett about Erica."

Although I had heard about the ball and the fight I had not been at that party. She did not seem to believe me. "Have it your way," she shrugged. We fell silent. I ordered a beer, which she insisted on paying for. "Have you heard from Brett lately?"

"Not since she left New York."

"Me neither." Although neither of us had seen Brett in at least two years, we continued to talk about her. We decided that most likely she had broken up with her girlfriend, and almost surely she was back on cocaine.

When the conversation had run its course, the woman said she was tired of this place and asked if I wanted to go a party.

"I don't know," I said. My interest in her was merely by association, because she had known Brett, whom I had been in love with years ago.

"Come on," she said. "This place sucks."

I looked around. The women were pigs. "All right," I said.

We got in a cab and headed uptown. We stopped in front of a very tall midtown building, the kind with doormen and elevatormen and expensive lobbies decorated in hideous taste. There was marble on the floor and mirrors on the walls, and you knew just what the apartment was going to look like when you got upstairs—inexpensive parquet, low ceilings, cheap "luxurious" fixtures that were already breaking.

A bunch of women were there. The music was loud. You could smell marijuana and there was plenty of liquor, but the drug they were really into was coke. This was before the lower classes had gotten hold of it and invented crack, so it was still fashionable. I went into the bathroom with Brett's friend as she chopped up some lines on the porcelain of the sink.

Usually coke is lousy and over-priced, but this stuff was very strong. I felt dizzy in a nice way, as if things were rushing at me. Brett's friend tried to kiss me, but I left the bathroom, to talk to the other women quickly before the coke wore off and I lost my personality.

People were looking at me with the same expressions I felt I was looking at them with. The whole thing was contrived and ridiculous, the way New York was contrived and ridiculous, with everybody spending tons of money to have a good time, yet nobody was having a good time. At the moment I was not actually depressed or bored; I was feeling alive and happy, but it was because of the coke, and I knew the feelings were invalid, or rather, the conclusions I was drawing from the feelings were invalid. I tried to remember the last time I had felt something real—all I could think of was acid.

I spotted two well-dressed women lounging in what seemed a bored fashion on a sofa. After looks got so complicated in the late seventies that it was impossible to tell who was attractive or not, I had begun to use clothing to guide me instead. In all my years of searching for women I have never been able to come up with a decent pick-up line, and tonight was no exception. "Hello," I said stupidly.

Although they looked at me without interest, I sat down next to them. I asked them their names and, when they didn't so much as ask me mine back, their professions.

"Real estate," said one.

"Commercial or—"

"Co-ops and condos." She looked around for someone more interesting to talk to, then stood up and asked the other woman if she wanted something to drink.

"What do *you* do?" I asked the other one, feeling like a polite mother talking to her friend's child.

"Media."

"Television, you mean?"

"In a manner of speaking."

I have always had trouble understanding what people in "media" actually do, and I decided this time I would really find out. "What exactly does that mean?" I asked.

"Well, for one thing, we're interested in developing ways to reach the kinds of people that aren't usually reached."

"Reached by what?"

"The usual methods."

"But what are they?"

"I'm not interested in that. That's the creative side."

"Then what are you interested in?"

"Jesus!" She yawned. As usual, I knew no more than when we had started. The real estate woman came back and she took a drink. Although they didn't say anything to each other, I felt excluded. I wasn't sure whether they were together or not. In any case, it seemed clear they wanted to talk to someone more interesting than me, so I left them.

The whole party was filled with people like this—account executives and media specialists who bought and sold "space," people who made commercials and marketing experts who advised them how to reach the target audience, art directors for "in-house" publications and technical advisers for corporate slide shows, grant writers and fundraisers and people who taught subjects like these in the "communications" departments of various colleges and universities. Sometimes it seemed like a couple hundred people in America did all the work—the real work of producing and creating things—and the rest just figured out ways to finance and promote and circulate them around. Despite the fact that nobody at the party seemed to have actually done anything, they all seemed to have a lot of money, which totally irritated me. I determined that, at the very least, I'd use up as much of their coke as possible. I told myself it was stupid to have come to this party; what else could I expect from a friend of Brett's?

I wandered around the room a bit more, but despite the coke, all my encounters were unsatisfactory. I began to feel more and more conscious of my clothing. It was okay for the bar, but it didn't work here. And yet I knew it wasn't just the clothing. There was a degree of hipness or cool here that my desires prevented me from achieving. I could try to mimic it, as I had mimicked other modes of acting in the past, but by the time I got the hang of it people would surely be into something else, and once again it would be too late. I didn't really like this hipness, but I also distrusted people who didn't have it, since there was something wrong with them—as there was something wrong with me.

The girl who had known Brett walked over. "Are you having a good time?" she asked.

"Okay," I shrugged.

"Would you like some more coke?"

"All right."

We went into the bedroom and sat down on the bed. She spread some coke on the cover of a book she picked up. I did some lines and then some other people did too. A bunch of women were lying on the bed. If I hadn't been on coke I would never have lain down but I didn't care what people thought so I lay back on the bed with them. No one seemed to think the situation was erotic except me. They were playing Whitney Houston and James Brown. I don't usually like black music but the sound system was very good and I began to get into it. I shut my eyes. I decided this was the real, the only music, the rest was white bread and I was white bread too. For some reason I felt happy and relaxed thinking this.

In spite of the coke I began to drift off. Maybe it wasn't to sleep but just to some strange kind of place. Then I became conscious of a pleasant sensation around my neck. It felt like someone was blowing on it. When things are good there's no sense changing anything, so I didn't open my eyes. At first I thought it might be accidental, but I shifted slightly and still I felt it. There had been a curly-haired woman near where I had lain down and I was hoping this was her. I didn't want her to know I was looking so I peeked secretly through my eyelashes.

It was not the attractive, curly-haired woman but a woman whom I remembered seeing in the other room. She was fat and unattractive and I was angry at myself for having peeked, because of course I'd have to make her stop. Then I decided I didn't have to make her stop; as long as no one knew she was doing this it was all right. I mean, it was all right as long as no one knew *I* knew she was doing this. Very gently her fat fingers were brushing the hairs on the back of my neck. I told myself it was okay because we were in a room with other people and nothing would happen between her and me. But it was very exciting to be getting aroused secretly in front of the other people— even if it was by someone fat and ugly. Then I realized that her fatness and ugliness were what was making this exciting.

She began brushing the inside of my thigh. This was dangerous because it was more visible. I sneaked another look through my eyelids but people were looking out the window at some stuff. Some people were asking the woman I had come to the party with about Brett. They talked about Miami real estate for a while, then went back to New York real estate. "Maybe we should leave them alone," someone said. It took me a moment to realize they were talking about the fat woman and me. I wanted to leave with them, to show them I wasn't the type of person who would have sex with a fat person, but I realized that if they had already noticed her doing stuff to me it was too late. I decided I'd wait until they left the room, then get up and sneak out of the party and go back to the bar.

I heard the door open, the women leave. "Enjoy your-self, Shirley," one of them said. Someone laughed, then I heard the door shut. She had stopped touching me when the women left and I was about to get up when I felt her push herself off the bed and heard her move to the door. I didn't want to look like I was following her so I stayed on the bed with my eyes shut as if I really was asleep. There was a click. Could it be possible that a fat woman named Shirley had abandoned me? Then I felt rather than heard her return to the bed and plump herself down. The indentation of her weight on the futon made me roll slightly towards her. She started in on my neck again. I told myself I'd get up when she stopped. Then I felt her other hand on my pants, on top of my vagina. A searing heat kind of thing went through me that was so powerful it was all I could do not to make a noise, though I breathed a bit deeply. She unbuttoned my pants. I put my hand there as if to push hers away. "Don't worry. I locked the door," she said.

Since nobody in the party would believe I hadn't known what was going on, I decided I might as well stay. I was extremely turned on. Surely this was due to the necessity of not showing my arousal to her in any way. Nor did I open my eyes. If she knew I knew what she looked like, I'd have to leave. She unzipped my pants and stuck her hand inside my underpants. It was tight because my pants made it hard for her to maneuver her hand. "Oooh," she said when she finally got there. I was very wet. She tried to get her hand inside me but my pants were too tight. "Raise your hips," she said, "so I can take these off." She tried to pull down my pants with her other hand but I was still pretending to be half asleep, so I wouldn't move my hips. "I see," she said. She took her hand out of my underpants and put one hand under my hips and lifted me as she pulled the pants down with the other. This is an awkward thing to do, so it took a long time. Finally the pants were around my legs. Then she crawled on top of me and pushed her tongue in my mouth. She weighed a lot but I had to let her. She pushed her tongue down my throat, around my gums, and slobbered on me. It was disgusting but I was in this posture of not knowing what was happening and if I told her to stop I'd be admitting I knew. Then she pushed up my shirt and began licking around my nipple. The licking was gentle like the thing on the neck had been and I no longer wanted her to stop. She moved rhythmically in a circle, and my body did too. I thought I heard her say, "Aha!" but I wasn't sure. As she continued to do this she shifted her weight so most of it was on my right side, then she put her hand back between my legs. "Oooh," she said. She took some goo and rubbed it on my thigh, then she lifted her tongue from my nipple and put the hand with my goo on it on my face. It felt like the sticky part of an egg. Her elbow dug into me as she supported herself. Then she lowered herself down my body. It felt heavy but somehow comfortable. She put her mouth around my nipple again but this time after a few gentle licks she began to bite. It hurt, but of course I couldn't say "ow." I tried to squirm but she held me down so I couldn't get away. Just when it was about to become too much she went back to the licks for a bit, and so on. She moved her hand back to my vagina. She flicked it a few times then put a finger inside me. "Spread your legs," she said. Although I wanted to I didn't. She moved my legs as far apart as she could with the pants still around my ankles, then she must have decided this wasn't enough, for she got off the bed, ripped off my shoes without even untying the laces, and pulled off my pants. She shoved my legs apart with both hands. She sat down between them and began pulling at the hairs around my vagina. She bit the inside of my thighs a few times, then put a finger in me. I moved to get it in deeper. Then she stuck two more fingers inside me. At first this felt good, but she spread me even farther apart and pushed even more deeply into me. It hurt a little, but in the right kind of way. Her hand was on my right leg as she balanced herself. She shoved her hand in and out as if we were fucking. It made an embarrassing sucking noise. I could hear it clearly because there was no more music in the room, though I could hear it in the party outside.

Then I felt a real pain. I couldn't tell exactly what was happening. First I thought she was trying to put her thumb inside me, then I decided she was curling her fingers into a fist. I felt like I could be split apart, but I told myself that babies' heads came out of there, it must be large enough. I heard myself making noise—"uh . . . uh . . ."—a kind of grunt. The upper part of my body rocked a bit, but she crawled on top of me to hold me down. I wanted to tell her she was really hurting me but the longer this went on the harder it was to talk. I told myself to relax, to let her hand in. She began sucking on my ear, then she dribbled into it. She licked my neck and I felt like a cat, arching it, then she began to suck. This was terrible because it would make a hickey but it seemed stupid to tell her to stop this when she was doing something much worse to my vagina. She began sucking right around the center of my throat and it was very ticklish but pleasant and when I stopped moving my neck I realized that her entire fist was inside me and my body had closed itself around her hand. I told myself to be careful how I moved so she wouldn't rip me apart. There was pain there but so much so it had become a kind of numbness so that I almost couldn't feel anything, and yet it was extremely satisfying, maybe because for once there was no place left to go. She knew all my secrets, at least all the secrets in this part of my body, which at the time seemed the only important thing. She spread her fist open a bit and I tried to breathe into the pain so we could be in it together. She moved her hand, and I breathed, then I felt a part of my body that had never been touched be touched. Through the walls of my vagina she was touching other organs. It was frightening but fascinating. It was like a tickle deep inside that you wanted to be scratched. But if she scratched she could break through and I could get peritonitis and die. It occurred to me how odd it would be if I got peritonitis from this fat woman whose last name I didn't even know, and died. What if there was dirt in her fingernails and they scraped my vagina? I felt I could scream from the tickling. As if she were reading my mind she spread the fist so the pain increased to balance the tickling and I could stand it. They cancelled each other out. Janis Joplin was singing ". . . take another little piece of my heart, baby" in the other room—a very clear version that I decided had to be a CD. It reminded me once again about dying. I had never heard of a woman dying from this and I decided I was just having an anxiety attack, like I did when I thought I couldn't breathe. I used to have them all the time when I had sex but I had kept breathing, hadn't I? But of course this woman might have lost all her judgment from coke. I didn't know if she had been doing coke or not. For all I knew she could have done some of that new blotter acid that was said to be going around and could be really nuts. For all I knew, Brett's friend had slipped blotter acid into my drink and *I* was the one who was nuts. For all I knew the whole thing had been planned as a setup for the fat woman.

"Try to relax," she said. "I'm coming out."

This hurt much more than her entering, because I wasn't so excited. I bit my lip to compensate for the pain—

the way her spreading her fist inside had compensated for the tickle—so I wouldn't say "ow."

The fist was out. I felt exhausted and depressed. Her breath smelled bad as she kissed me. The whole thing seemed stupid and dangerous and far away.

She was off me. I suddenly realized how hard it had been to breathe. The gunk on my body began to evaporate and I felt cold. The bed rose a little as she stood up. I heard her moving around. I assumed she was straightening herself up. As soon as she left I would get dressed and leave the party. The only person who knew me here was Brett's friend; if I were lucky she had already gone home.

"Open your eyes." If I hadn't while her fist was forcing its way into my body, I sure wasn't going to now. "Come on, open your eyes." I could feel the bed sinking under her weight again. "Or I'll take your pants into the other room."

I opened my eyes. Now that I was no longer excited, she seemed even worse than when I had glimpsed her through my eyelashes. She leaned forward to kiss me but I turned aside my head.

Her hand was on my nipple. I tried to push it away but she pinched it tightly. "Ow," I said, since my eyes were open.

"Ow, my ass! You little slut," she said. We stared at each other, registering the disgust in each other's eyes. Without another word she left the room.

I sat up, pulled on my pants, and bent down to look for my shoes. As I straightened up I heard a click, then the smell of gas, then the sound and smell of paper being burned.

I turned around. Brett's friend was sitting there, in a chair, puffing contentedly on a cigarette.

"Have a good time?" she asked.

"I was asleep," I said.

"The fuck you were."

I dressed myself as quickly as I could so I could leave the room with her, but she left while I was still combing my hair. "Brett'll get a kick out of this," she said with a mean little smile as she opened the door.

When I left the room I felt the people at the party were all talking about me and what I had done, but perhaps I was making this up. There was coke all around me, and although I needed it to make me able to stand myself I was afraid they'd tell me I couldn't have it, that I'd gone beyond the compact we had all implicitly made only to sleep with attractive people and had to be punished for it.

As I searched for my coat, I saw the fat woman I had had sex with laughing with some people in the kitchen. They looked at me in disgust as I walked past them. It didn't seem fair. If it was disgusting for me to have sex with her because she was fat, why wasn't it disgusting for them to be friends with her?

Although I felt awful, I took a cab back to the bar. There was no way I could stand being alone with myself that night. Not that I was worse than anybody else; in fact, I felt I was better, because I was more honest. But it was this honesty that made me unable to stand myself, so I had to go back to the bar, whereas stupid people like Brett and her friend were able to do things much worse and laugh it off without a second thought.

"Back again?" said the coat check girl.

"Lousy party." As usual, I felt embarrassed to be alone in the bar at this hour, especially in front of the coat check girl, who had seen me alone so many nights through the years. And yet, the fact that I had seen the coat check girl alone through the years did not make her an object of pity to me, even though I had never seen her pick anyone up, or even seen anyone who might be a lover hanging around the coat check area waiting for her to get off work. As she took my coat and hung it up I realized I didn't even pity her for her terrible job. On the contrary, I felt in some weird way she was a privileged person in the hierarchy of the bar whom it was necessary to keep on my side.

I call her "girl" but really she was a woman, maybe ten years older than me. She was short and kind of tough looking, yet on certain nights I would have been desperate enough to go home with her, if she had come on to me. But she had never come on to me, and, of course, I had never come on to her. It is possible coat check girls are told not to come on to anyone, or perhaps it is implicit in this kind of job.

She never seemed to wonder what I thought about her, or what anyone else thought about her, and I wondered how this could be. If I were a coat check girl I would constantly be wondering what people thought about my humiliating job—if they thought I took it as a way to pick people up, or not be alone in the evening. And yet I didn't think of this particular coat check girl as being humiliated by her job. If anyone pitied anyone it seemed to be her pitying me, when she saw me go home alone or with someone unattractive. When I left with someone attractive I always tried to make sure she saw it, even in the summer when the person I was with might not have a coat.

I ordered a beer, then sat down at the bar. It was almost three, and the women that were still there were pretty drunk. Bars tend to be interesting at that hour. You can see the realm of people's possibilities narrowing before your eyes, so a person they would scorn to go home with at two-thirty becomes acceptable by three, and quite desirable by three-thirty.

Unfortunately, the coke had made it impossible for me to be drunk, so I was in a different head from everybody else. Things were clear and bright, if a little slow, and this slowness made it more boring than it would have been otherwise. I told myself to concentrate on the formal qualities of the language around me.

"Yes you do."

"No I don't."

"Yes you do."

"Come on, Shelley, *stop* it."

"What's Maria gonna say?"

"What's Maria gonna know?"

"I have to tell her."

"Says who?"

"I have to tell her. You know that. I just have to tell her."

"I don't know that."

"I have to tell her."

"See that chick over there? She's so hot."

"The one with the hair? You got to be kidding."

I watched the girl walk across the room and start to talk to the person with the hair. I looked at her friend, who was probably in love with her. I wondered if when they looked at me they thought I was someone like them. I wished I could be someone like them, the people you read about in the *Post*.

"What're you staring at?" the friend said.

"Nothing." I turned away. The coat check girl was sitting on her stool, staring into space. I felt a sudden empathy with her. I imagined her loneliness, so much greater than mine, and decided to do her a favor.

I walked over. "How's it going?" I asked.

"Okay. Same as usual."

"You like working here?"

She nodded. "It's convenient. I like the people."

We fell silent. I wondered how to bring the subject up. Then I thought of the embarrassment of waiting for her and walking out the door with her. Everyone who worked at the bar would know. I decided I'd leave first, and she could come over after work.

"So you're a friend of Brett's?" she asked.

"Yeah."

"How's she like Miami?"

"Pretty good," I said. "She's got a white convertible. She says she realizes that's what she always wanted."

She laughed. "That's Brett for you."

I looked at her. Although unattractive, she had a warmth about her that would be useful in assuaging my self-disgust. But I had to speak to her now, before the coke was completely out of my system.

"I'm tired," I said.

"You want your coat?"

"I spose." She handed me my coat. "You could spend the night with me," I said.

She laughed. "No I couldn't."

"Why not? What else are you gonna do?"

"What I always do. Go home."

A couple came up and I waited until she gave them their coats. As soon as they left I started in again. Her refusal had piqued my interest. "Is it that you think you don't know me well enough, or maybe you know me too well?"

"Too well! You've been coming here, what, ten years? I bet you don't even know my name."

She was right. "I've gone home with plenty of people I didn't know their names," I protested. But I told her my name and then asked her for hers. "So will you come over or what?"

She laughed. "No."

"Why the fuck not?" After the night I had had, I felt I deserved at least this.

"For one thing, my lover wouldn't like it."

"Oh." I hated the way I said it, as if in disappointment. It soothed my ego in terms of this night, but it was worse in the long run to think this unattractive woman had a lover and I didn't.

"You been together long?" I asked idly.

"Twelve years."

"Twelve years!"

"That's nothing. I was with my previous lover sixteen years."

I tried to figure out how many nights this was, nights when she wasn't alone and I was: probably somewhere between eight or nine thousand. God knows what her lover looked like, but then, how unattractive did a person have to be not to make that worthwhile. "Jesus. How old are you?"

"Forty-six."

"That's impossible!"

"Not if you start very young."

"Boy!" I tried to digest this. "She doesn't mind your staying out so late every night?"

"Uh-uh."

"The tolerant type, huh?"

"Not really. She's up late too."

"What does she do?"

She tilted her head towards the bar. "Tends bar."

"Judy?" She was the fat, nice one.

"Chrissie."

"Chrissie!" I exclaimed. Chrissie was the "beautiful"

bartender—beautiful in the way that people who serve you, if you see them often enough, become beautiful. She had blond hair and a few freckles, and even if she hadn't worked at this bar I wouldn't have thrown her out of my bed.

"Yeah, Chrissie," she said smugly, as if she knew what I had been thinking.

"God!" So that she wouldn't misinterpret—actually, interpret correctly—my astonishment that she was sleeping with Chrissie, I transferred it to her age. "She looks so young. If you've been together all that time she must be in her thirties."

"Thirty-two."

I shook my head. "That's amazing! All these years I've been coming to this bar, and I've seen her, and I've seen you, and I never knew."

"I'll bet there's things even more amazing than that that you don't know," she said.

padova

A long time ago, when I was still young and confused about life, my apartment burned down. Everything was gone—my dog, my cat, my books, my typewriter: only the pages of my first novel, bound tightly together in their springboard binder, were spared, their edges but slightly charred. This seemed ironic, for no one would publish that book. It took a while for the pain of my losses to hit, so caught up was I in the miseries of an unrequited love. I wandered around, trying to buy stuff to wear, waiting for the loved one to call. But as hard as it is to buy things when you need nothing, it is harder when you need everything, and I found it simpler to wear the second-hand clothing friends gave me. Soon even I began to notice I was acting oddly. I rarely bathed, and I was angry at anyone who had more possessions than me—in those days, before the homeless, everyone. Despite this I instantly accumulated a variety of lovers, drawn perhaps by my detachment, perhaps by my anger, perhaps, for all I know, my lack of bathing. A month later it all collapsed. I stopped acting like a rabbit, and began to fall asleep—"pass out" is perhaps more like it—at the slightest approach to my genitalia. Soon a vague depression enveloped not just my current but also, in retrospect, my past life. Not only wasn't I happy, I had never been happy, and I would never be happy. Nor did I deserve to be happy. Look at the people in China, Latin America, the Soviet Union, people in prison, being tortured, dying of painful diseases, paralyzed in car crashes: what did I have to complain about? Soon I did nothing but lie on the bed all day in a kind of haze, dreading the moment when my official girlfriend would come home and try to put her hand into my body. All this, of course, only made me hate myself even more.

I had been like this for several months when my father offered me a trip to Europe. He's the kind of person who believes doing things can perk you up. I dreaded going, but I dreaded staying even more. Plus, it would help with a career change I had decided upon. Unable to write, and jealous of the more glamorous lives of my artist friends, I had decided to become a painter, or perhaps a sculptor, maybe even one of those new performance artists. Minimalism was still around at this time—huge canvases covered with nothing but gray or white paint—so I figured my lack of drawing skills wouldn't be a hindrance. Worse come to worst, I could project a slide on a canvas and airbrush a copy, like those crazy painters whose work looked like photographs. Armed with an excellent art guidebook, I headed, therefore, to Italy.

It had been years since I had been to Europe, and at first I was deeply disappointed. Milan was just like New York, but more so. For a day or so I did nothing but lie in bed reading *The Last Picture Show*, feeling nostalgic for an America I had seen only from an airplane. But gradually I realized my father was right. For the first time in months I felt in control of my life. No one knew where I was, my decisions were simple and concrete—where to eat, what hotel to stay in and for how long—and I could send as many postcards to the unrequiting one as I liked.

One of the things I most wanted to do was attend the opera in Verona, where works were performed outdoors in an old Roman amphitheater that even after several thousand years still managed to have better acoustics than Lincoln Center's recently acoustically remodeled (for the third or fourth time) Avery Fisher Hall. But when I arrived there I found the festival didn't start for a few more days, so I decided to catch it on my way back from Venice. Venice, at least, would surely satisfy my craving for foreignness. Finding myself in a city that looked like a child's birthday cake, I tried to persuade myself I was happy. I partially succeeded, even though I ended up taking my gondola ride alone. Americans were all around, but I didn't know how to strike up a conversation with them: in their boisterous good humor they seemed more foreign than the Italians. I would sit next to them in restaurants, contemptuous of their taste, envious of their personalities, eagerly overhearing their English.

Each night when I came back to my pensione, near where the Grand Canal empties into the sea, the concierge, Signor Delponte, would offer me a grappa. After this he would offer me himself. As he was an unattractive man in his fifties and I was a not unattractive woman almost thirty years his junior, even he must have seen that the offer had little appeal on the surface, and after a night or two he began to offer additional inducements: a second grappa, a free breakfast (the pensione served no food), once, oddly, some porno photographs. These were black-and-white, grainy pictures of unattractive people doing unattractive and not particularly exciting things to each other, and I could not understand why Signor Delponte imagined they could be the way to a young American's heart—or even body. I suggested he would do better offering free dinners or a reduction—even negation—of the bill. He pondered the latter a while before making a grudging offer of a twenty-percent discount. Rather grateful I had not been tempted by a full cancellation of the bill (a week's stay in Venice can be expensive), I explained that the suggestion had been meant not for myself but for others. This did not discourage his pestering in the least, and when he asked for the fifth or sixth time whether or not I was interested in women, I did not deny it, despite the salaciousness I feared this might inspire. He asked me if I had met any women in Italy. I told him no, not yet, but I had the name of a bar in Rome.

The next day, when I returned from la Scuola Tintoretto, Signor Delponte was standing in front of the pensione with an attractive man in his mid-forties. Signor Delponte made a point of introducing him to me; from his suit alone you could tell he was of a much higher social class than the concierge. Carlo was driving the next morning to Padova, where the concierge had told him I was headed; I could travel with him if I wanted. Clearly this encounter had been arranged, and although it made me nervous I nonetheless accepted; at the very least it would save me train fare, and possibly the cost of lunch and some taxi rides as well. I had been planning to spend a few hours in the afternoon seeing the famous Giotto frescoes in Padova before taking the train on to Verona so I could finally catch the opera.

That night over our farewell grappa Signor Delponte began making insinuations about this drive. My suspicions confirmed, I told him I had changed my mind and decided to go by myself on the train. I didn't know Carlo and I had had my share of unpleasant experiences with Italian men who acted as if a female American tourist—at least one traveling alone—was by definition a whore. Distressed, Signor Delponte assured me I had nothing to worry about. Carlo was a wealthy man who held a major soft-drink bottling franchise for all of northern Italy; his purpose in driving to Padova was to see his girlfriend, a young and beautiful woman who did not confine her sexual interests exclusively to the persons of one gender. The ride itself, in the most expensive kind of Citroen, the one that floated on a cushion of air, would certainly be faster and more comfortable than the train.

A warmth in my lower torso, which I had not experienced in months, went through me like a wave; I gratefully accepted a second grappa.

In the morning I took a long bath. Although it seemed likely I wouldn't be highly attracted to Carlo's girlfriend (Italians were the opposite of the Nordic blondes I then preferred), the idea of the adventure appealed to me— the kind of thing one might read about in a novel. I paid my bill and sat down to wait for Carlo in the lobby of the pensione. He was late, and after a while I told Signor Delponte that I was going to take the vaporetto to the station. He protested vehemently that Carlo would come; if by any chance the plans had been changed he would certainly still drive me to Padova. As we were arguing a motorboat taxi approached. Carlo grabbed my luggage and I thanked the concierge for all his kind services.

To my surprise, Carlo didn't speak any English, so we stumbled along in a mixture of Italian and French, the latter of which he knew scarcely better than me. He told me he was married, with two children who went away with his wife every summer to their vacation home in Sardinia; he joined them there on the weekends. His girlfriend was twenty-two and lived—as unmarried women in Italy then did—with her parents. The plan was for Carlo and me to have an early lunch together, then meet the girlfriend at her apartment when she came home from work during the siesta. At last I understood the purpose of those long Italian lunches.

In my nervousness—what if I didn't like her? what if she didn't like me?—I drank too much with my meal. Useful as this may have been for my libido, it was terrible for my linguistic ability. I began to confuse Italian and French, then bits of Spanish crept in too. I began to get irritated with Carlo for not understanding me—he was European, wasn't he?—whereas I was merely an American who wasn't supposed to be able to speak anything but English. Some people said Americans didn't even speak English. "*Sì, sì*," he said, "*tu es americana. Capito.*"

My image of Italian women was stereotypical: short, dark mother figures with huge breasts, occasionally beautiful like Sophia Loren, but far more likely to be loaded with hair and other unpleasant characteristics—really, not my type at all. So you can imagine my delight when a tall, thin, red-haired woman in a full-length, half-opened robe opened the door. *Of course*, I told myself, a man who held a major soft-drink bottling franchise in northern Italy could afford any woman he chose. She gave a huge smile when she saw me, and began talking about me to Carlo. "*Che bellisima!*" she kept exclaiming. "*Tu es tres bella anche*," I told her.

She looked at me puzzled. Carlo translated for me. She told him to tell me there was a bidet down the hall to the right. I said it was unnecessary, I had had a *bagno* this morning, but she insisted. As I went off, they laughed and I heard the word *americana*.

When I returned she led me to the bedroom and began to undress me. After I was naked she had me turn slowly around, as tailors who shortened my skirts back when I was in school had done. On occasion her hands lightly moved parts of my body one way or the other, not sexually but as if I were a model she was trying to place in a good position. She and Carlo were both still dressed, and I found this impersonal inspection of my body extremely arousing. The American women I had slept with were either lesbians who were still embarrassed by their attraction to women or feminists who pretended that the reason they slept with women was not sexual but ideological; this casual acceptance of the carnality of our transaction seemed to me the essence of European sophistication.

Then Francesca (for that was her name) undid her robe and pulled me onto the bed. She was taller than me and it took a while for us to get our bodies properly aligned. She stopped often to make comments and jokes to Carlo —comments and jokes I knew were about me, but which I couldn't quite grasp. I didn't really mind, for they seemed well-intentioned. Carlo, now naked, joined us on the bed and began stroking my thighs. It was exciting, but when he turned me over as if to enter me I told him no, he could not *entrare*. Unlike most Italian men, he did not act as if "no" were a code word meaning "yes."

Francesca took her fingers, wet from my insides, and shoved them into my mouth. No one had done this to me before, and I wasn't sure whether the purpose was to excite me or just to let me know what I tasted like. I began

to suck her fingers as if they were a cock. She took them
out of my mouth and again put them inside my body,
then she held up her fingers to Carlo. He didn't lick them,
but they laughed; they seemed fascinated by my great
wetness. I explained to them I had had *una problema* and
had been unable to make love for a long time and now
that I could it was very exciting. The word *"problema"*
seemed to upset Francesca and I tried to explain that the
kind of problem I meant was of the head rather than the
body, that my apartment had burned down and I had
become sick—that is, tired—of the life. They looked at me
uncomprehendingly, and I realized I was speaking not so
much Italian as French or English or even Spanish with
an Italian syntax and accent.

Francesca had started out as the aggressor, but my
natural instincts of politesse and reciprocity took over, so
I began to lower myself down her body until my head was
stationed between her legs. Despite my occasional doubts
in other domains, I had none here, in the dark, with my
eyes shut. I scarcely paid attention as their voices continued
unobtrusively in the background, an incomprehensible
melange full of "oh's" and "ah's" as pleasant as the drone
of the lawn mowers and propeller planes that used to fill
the sky on lazy summer afternoons at my grandmother's.
I felt happier and more comfortable than I had in ages—
partially on account of the revival of my sexual desire, but
even more, I think, because of the exoticness of the
situation. I imagined both the story I would tell my friends
and the one I would write about this, how I would try to
describe the aging apartment with the bidet in the bathroom, its mirrored wardrobes instead of closets, its high
ceilings and wooden shutters, and also the way I liked not
understanding what was being said—the subservient but
not unpleasant feeling of being a kind of toy for these two

grownups, one of whom was nonetheless younger than me.

After a while Francesca pushed me away. She had been making much noise but due to the difference in local customs and the shortness of our acquaintance it was impossible for me to tell whether or not she had come. I assumed she had, and was waiting for her to return the favor, but instead she spread her legs so Carlo could enter her. I tried to kiss her as she made love to Carlo, but she paid no attention to me, and eventually I just lay back and watched. Francesca seemed more excited by Carlo than she had been by me, and I realized, with the slight surprise that always accompanies such revelations, that there really were women who liked men better than women—better even than a woman as remarkable as myself. It occurred to me I might have been brought there less for Francesca's sake than for Carlo's.

When they were done she disappeared into the bathroom. I could hear the water running; when she returned she began dressing for work. Carlo also took a shower. They offered me one but I said no, I would take one later that evening. They looked at me oddly. I tried to explain how I wanted her smell with me all that afternoon, but although my languages had returned somewhat I couldn't be sure they understood what I meant.

Carlo suggested I spend the night with them in Padova, but I was still determined to get to Verona so I could see the opera. Already I had missed the first night of the festival. I asked for Francesca's phone number in case I was ever in town again. She seemed reluctant to give it to me, and told me to hang up if her mother answered. When I tried to kiss her goodbye she laughed and hugged me, as if to make sure I did not put my tongue in her mouth.

I had Carlo drop me off at the station, where I checked my luggage before walking to the church where the frescoes were. The train was leaving soon and I didn't have much time to see the Giottos. They were his most famous work, the link between medieval painting and the Renaissance, and I knew from the guidebook the ways in which they should be appreciated. But even as I sketched them in my notebook, memories of the afternoon kept floating through my mind. A voice kept telling me how stupid I was: what was an opera compared to spending the night with Carlo and Francesca—a woman perhaps more beautiful than any I, in my then limited experience, had ever slept with? I told myself I was a phony: my parents and my official girlfriend thought of me as a free spirit, but it was merely that I was as rigid in my amusements as ordinary people were in their work. Just think how I went around Italy: coordinating museum and church hours and train schedules, shlepping miles to eat in whatever restaurants the guidebook told me to, diligently searching out famous paintings in transepts and naves. (What was a transept? what was a nave?) Who in New York was working harder than me? With these thoughts in mind I headed back to the train station, where I learned that, most uncharacteristically, I had missed my train. The next one wasn't leaving till almost nine, which meant I would again miss the opera.

Verona wasn't far, and I determined to hitch. This was the early seventies, when such modes of travel were acceptable—admirable, even. I envied the backpackers their freedom and courage and ability to live on almost nothing, perhaps because I knew I could never do this myself.

I took a taxi to the highway and put my bags down and my thumb out. Almost immediately a convertible with two young men in it pulled up. I started to get in, but they made several comments that even I, with my limited Italian, could understand, and I gave them the finger as they sped away. Other cars stopped, but it was more of the same. I decided to hold out for a woman.

Time went by. The sun was setting, the wine from lunch was getting to me. I was so tired I felt I could lie down on the grass by the side of the road and fall asleep. Finally a middle-aged man stopped. He was not a woman, but with his black suit and gray-flecked beard he reminded me of a Hasidic Jew, and I felt I would be safe with him. He told me he was going to a little town right near Verona. *"Quanti kilometri?"* I asked. In English he asked me if I spoke English. I assured him I did; with relief I placed my bags in the back seat of the car and got in next to him.

We drove a few miles in silence, then abruptly he pulled the car over to the side of the road. He put his hand on my leg.

"No," I said, removing his hand. He grabbed my hand with his other one and with the first started to unzip my jeans. I tried to use my other hand to stop him but of course he was stronger than me. The smell of garlic, which had made me keep my head turned towards the window as we drove, grew quite nauseating.

"Sono menstruanda," I told him—*"sangue."* I realized I was still thinking of him as a Hasid. No Orthodox Jew would go near a woman with her period (so I thought at the time) and other men weren't so crazy about blood either.

He looked at me a moment, then took his hand away from my pants. For a second I thought I was saved. Then he unzipped his pants and looked at me expectantly, then at the door. The message was clear. Either I did something to his penis or I had to get out of the car.

I looked out the window. It was almost dark. I didn't know where I was. I had left Padova and a beautiful woman all for the purpose of attending the opera in Verona this night. I was very tired, a little scared, and still somewhat aroused from the afternoon's adventure. Who knew what was in store for me if I got out of the car—or was this just a lie I told myself to excuse my behavior?

I put my hand on his penis and asked him, if I did this, would he drive me to Verona? He nodded his head, and I felt almost grateful, both for the ride and the fact that I did not have to put my mouth on his genitals. He was repugnant to me—lower-class, smelling of garlic, nowhere near as attractive as Carlo, whom I had turned down just a few hours ago—but I found it easy to distance myself, as I had found it easy to distance myself from my fire, as I had found it easy to distance myself from the woman in New York who did not love me (and from the woman in New York who loved me, as well), as I had distanced myself from my friends in high school, staring at their naked, unsuspecting bodies in the girls' locker room. After he came he zipped up his pants and got back on the highway and continued with his part of the bargain. Despite his disgustingness, my body felt on fire, and I was almost sorry I had told him I had my period.

I had him drop me at the hotel I had stayed in the previous week, and I asked the proprietor where I could get tickets for the opera. "*Opera?*" he said. "*Domani.*" I looked at the schedule in disbelief; could I, who never made mistakes, be wrong for the second time this day? No, there it was, *Un Ballo in Maschera*, July 22–24. It was the twenty-third. I was safe.

The proprietor shook his head; the opera was yesterday and tomorrow, not today. Not believing him, I left my bags in my room and walked over to the amphitheater.

But he was right. A dash in Italy did not mean what it meant in America. The opera was the twenty-second and the twenty-fourth. I had missed it again.

In immense frustration I called Padova; perhaps I could go back and see Francesca, or Francesca and Carlo—or even just Carlo; by that point I was so angry and frustrated anyone would have done. But an older woman picked up the phone, and after much incomprehensible chatter I learned that Francesca was out. At least that's what I think she said, but just as easily it may have been that no one of that name was there, and I had been given a wrong number.

I ate dinner in an outdoor restaurant on the square. It was crowded, and when I left even more men than usual grabbed at me. If someone had been polite I might have responded, but they just made the standard stupid comments. For once I couldn't even make myself angry. I felt that I had been putting out a strange odor ever since that morning, an odor that drew men to me like dogs.

When I returned to my hotel there were several cars out front, each with a woman of uncertain age wearing too much makeup inside it. The women smoked their cigarettes and chatted idly with each other out their open windows. *Le puttane*, I thought, I won't even have to take a bath. I approached the nearest one and asked, "*Quanta costa?*" She seemed puzzled. I pulled out my wallet and pointed to the hotel. I said I had a room there and asked how much she charged, by the hour and the night.

She looked at me in disbelief, then rolled up the window on my side and shouted something out the other window to the whores. They laughed at me in a way that had no friendliness about it. Their laughter followed me into the hotel, and I could not shake my mind of the thought that once I had gone upstairs, they would tell the proprietor of my peculiar request. All night I imagined I could hear them laughing in the square, the laughter rolling from one car to another, of whores who thought they were too good for the American, at the American who thought she was too good for the whores.

The next morning, hungover and exhausted and depressed, I checked out of the hotel and headed for the train station, where I discovered I had left my sketchbook at the hotel. Due to *le puttane* I didn't have the nerve to go back and get it, and I soon took this loss as a sign to give up my idea of becoming an artist. But somehow this made my failure to spend a night with Francesca and Carlo in Padova even more irritating. I regretted it deeply for weeks, and I was still thinking about it as I flew into a Tel Aviv airport surrounded with barbed wire and guarded by soldiers—for this was the summer that Israeli athletes were slaughtered in Munich, and an Israeli plane blown up in Tokyo in what was the beginning of a new age of terror. The world had finally and truly become foreign to me, but it was in a way I was not expecting and so I did not notice it: in the innocence and narcissism of my youth I was more interested in the woman I was moving towards and the girl I'd left behind.

key west

I was in Key West, partly as a reward for finishing a book, partly to escape from my lover. I didn't like her, but in my lazy way I had been faithful. I felt like a prisoner let out of jail. The air had a gentle breeze with the smell of the sea in it, as if you were sitting on a boat tied up in the harbor, and the streets were filled with the kinds of people you find on pieces of land that sit at the ends of continents, where there's nothing around you but water, and nowhere to go but far away. Far away is difficult to get to, so you stay, and much of your thought concerns the places you'll go to when the energy and the money come together, and even as you think about the possibilities, time disappears, until all of a sudden you realize you are old and the decision has already been made. People complain, but it's what makes these places interesting, the disappearance of time, in a way that relates not just to you personally but to the world outside, so that you can still find men with bandanas on their hair and beads on their necks eating avocado sandwiches next to fishermen, college brats on their spring vacation, and local factory girls looking to be carried away by northerners to someplace where seasons and sequence still exist, where life is a matter more serious than boats and fish and music and drugs.

Where I came from life was serious, and I liked the change. I was at a time in my life when I wanted to defeat time, and Key West was trying to do this, though of course it couldn't; it was merely hiding its passage behind food, tan, and air. Who knew that even then a virus was beginning to make its way through the beautiful bodies, a virus that would eventually bring seasons and death even to this place?

Overhead there were radio waves from the naval base singing through the night to our ships and planes vast and complex songs of location and weather and ways to respond to all sorts of potential catastrophes. Supposedly this was the greatest concentration of such radio waves in the world and it was said that the brain distortions caused by the constant bombardment of these waves was the source of the peculiar lackadaisicalness of the town, but I found the reasons both more historical and banal—a standard island mix of beach- and boat bums, hippie dropouts, and men who liked to spend their day throwing hooks with pieces of dead fish stuck in them in the water.

During the day I swam by the pier where people like myself swam, careful to take off my jewelry so as not to tempt the barracuda. I could not blame them for liking silver; I did too. At night I'd eat my stone crabs and rock shrimp on the verandas of Victorian houses where the waiters were handsomer than movie stars, wishing I would meet a woman who owned a house by the ocean, so that I would not have to go back to where life was serious and difficult and boring. I wanted to disappear, leaving papers and typewriter and winter clothing behind, and assume a new character and being, one having to do with music and boats and fish and marijuana—the way I wanted, when I was young, to wake up one day and suddenly find myself a cheerleader in Scarsdale. It was too late to be a cheerleader in Scarsdale, and perhaps it was too late for this too, and perhaps, after all, I didn't really want it. But I liked pretending I wanted it. As for my lover, she existed only in the context of New York. I could scarcely remember to call her, and when I did the concerns of her life—our old life—seemed as odd as African tribal customs. Who cared about the new dance company from Germany, the French filmmaker, the performance artist who lived chained to a tree in the middle of Central Park? She asked when was I coming back, should she buy tickets for the premiere of that avant-garde opera, the one that lasted for ten hours and had no music? I told her not to talk to me about time, it was my enemy, I was much more interested in what I was having for dinner. We had a fight but I didn't care, not when I was eating fish whose tails had slapped the water that very day, and all there was to do when you were done was meander in the downtown boutiques until the bars got busy—the bars that catered to the beautiful waiters, the guilty college boys, the men who craved them, and women like me.

I did not mind taking second place to the men; they were so handsome it's a wonder we didn't fall in love with them ourselves. They wore shirts with bright patterns on them that they left half-unbuttoned, shorts or loose white pants that let the air inside the way djellabas do; when they danced they moved like flowers in a hurricane. The women in their tight pants, gold-colored jewelry, and lipstick dressed like Puerto Ricans, but if their skin was dark it was more likely due to the sun, the sun that darkened their skin and lightened their hair. Like fish, they hung out mostly in groups, and I felt conspicuous in a not especially good way being there among them by myself, as if I were pathetic and had no friends. Men could get away with this—men could get away with anything—but I felt like I was in a college where everyone was in a sorority but me. I felt self-conscious if I had to push my way through them to order a beer, and when I had my beer I was uncertain whether to put it in a glass or not, or walk around with it or sit on the veranda or lean against the bar, and I kept thinking that when I got up and went to the bathroom they were talking about me. It was hard to look at them, and absurd to keep looking away. I told myself that when I was in New York with my friends we did not make fun of anyone just because they were in a bar alone, that it didn't matter whether I drank beer out of a bottle or a glass, that even I, who was so particular, had never used that particular discrimination as a basis for accepting or rejecting anyone. But I could not help remembering I used methods of discrimination, and that just because I had never used that particular one it didn't mean nobody else ever did. I knew also that what was really significant was not whether I used a bottle or a glass but how I handled this decision, and this was where I failed; it was my self-consciousness concerning this that made me conspicuous. I told myself to stop being self-conscious, and hauled the bottle up to my mouth; in my haste some of it spilled on my shirt. I looked up to see someone looking at me, and though I felt like killing myself, I calmly asked the bartender for a napkin and a glass.

I told myself I should just make my decision—bottle or glass—and stick to it no matter what. If I did this consistently I would lose my self-consciousness, and if I were conspicuous it would be for other reasons (because I was good-looking or famous or sexy, for example), reasons that most people would enjoy—though not me, for I really don't enjoy being conspicuous. Perhaps I'm the only person in America who feels this way. What I like is being invisible, unnoticed and transparent as life goes on about me, and there is nothing to do but listen and watch.

I told myself I needed to dance. Only dancing could clear my mind. Five minutes of sweat and I would be all right.

I walked to the part of the dance floor where the women were. Someone moderately unattractive was standing alone against the bar, someone unattractive enough so that I didn't have to worry about her turning me down, and I asked her to dance.

She refused. She was tired, her head ached, her girl-friend was in the bathroom. I looked around to see if anyone had noticed my humiliation. It didn't seem like they had, but I felt this was not because they hadn't been watching but because out of a sort of discretion that had been triggered by my spilling of the beer they had all turned away until I could be comfortable in my body once again.

I went back to the bar, the outdoors one where there were tables and chairs filled with happy groups—people so tanned and relaxed it was clear they were not tourists but locals. They greeted each other by names and wavings as they flitted from table to table, exchanging gossip about their dinners, their lovers, their boats. The men had that nasal, knowing intonation, that high-pitched, almost hysterical laugh; the women, banal and serious even in their jokes, were like suburbanites discussing the particulars of how to run the annual golf tournament. To be outside of all this was like being a dork in high school, though in my intellectual New York high school to have been like them was to have been the dork. Now I was a grown-up and I still didn't know who was really the dork. I felt they were staring at me with a mixture of curiosity and (deserved) hostility, that they all knew I was just pretending to be a woman, that only out of the greatest kindness were they pretending they didn't know my secret, so I could continue to think it was still a secret. Very casually I turned and looked in the mirror over the bar to reassure myself that I was still a woman.

I told myself I didn't care if they were looking at me, that in spite of my shyness it was better to be conspicuous than invisible; in a way I was even proud of it. It showed I could not be invisible even if I wanted to, that no matter what I did a power would emanate out of me that would cause people to notice me. I felt I had endured things other people hadn't and couldn't, and I believed it was this even more than my brains that made me admirable, that I had suffered immense deprivations and that these had strengthened me even as they had permanently warped me. When I thought of people who had truly suffered immense deprivations these thoughts embarrassed me and I felt that in my pride about my tiny deprivations I was far more guilty than those who had never suffered a thing, but I also felt my guilt (and my suffering due to this guilt) was unfair, that it was a result of thought and effort and that the world was badly arranged if someone should be cursed—*especially* cursed, that is—just because she made an effort to use her brain. I didn't feel I deserved anything special because of my brain, but I felt that my efforts—not just mine but anyone's—should be rewarded. My biggest effort was suffering, and I probably felt unduly vain about this.

These mental gyrations—or perhaps it was merely the effect of the sun—made me tired, and after the second beer I went back to my hotel. I couldn't sleep, of course; the sugar from the alcohol and the beat of the music kept throwing images past my mind. I went out on the balcony and tried to listen to the waves. I realized after a while there were no waves, it was the sound of the cars driving out to the naval base.

The next night I went home with someone who worked at Pantry Pride. She was blond and trashy-looking so I should have liked her but somehow she was the wrong kind of trash. Her job was unpacking merchandise from boxes in the basement of Pantry Pride which a teenager would then put on the shelves. We had sex for an hour and a half and then she left; she couldn't spend the night because she had a child. After she left it occurred to me maybe she didn't really have a child but a lover, whom she had to get home to. But she had asked to see me the next night, so maybe she didn't have a lover after all.

I was pleased she'd asked to see me again because I felt I hadn't been very good in bed: I had not had the energy to invent a story in which she would be someone I really wanted to be in bed with.

Because I had told her I was busy and couldn't see her, the next night I went to the other gay bar. It was down the street a few blocks from the one I usually went to, and not many people were there. No doubt it would get busier later, but I liked it as it was, a few couples dancing lackadaisically on the dance floor, a half-empty garden outside, where several groups of women and one lone male couple were talking quietly to each other. The absence of people made it easier to be invisible, and my self-consciousness began to disappear. I told myself it did not matter whether I drank beer out of a bottle or a glass, I did not have to come to any decision, I could do what I wanted on the spur of the moment. This seemed immensely freeing—a principle I could use, not just in relation to whether to drink beer out of a bottle or a glass, but about other things as well.

I sat for a long time without moving, imagining the people who could be there—beautiful women in white dresses and beads who would instantly recognize me for what I was—and I was almost as happy as if they had been there. I told myself I was perverse, very unusual, that I had perhaps the most interesting thoughts of anyone on earth.

If this were true it would be terrible, because then there would be nobody on earth interesting enough for me to talk to.

I thought, as I often do in such circumstances, about God: the immense sorrow of God, eternal witness to entropy and death; the immense loneliness of God, who had no one to confide in or love; the immense boredom of God, who knew everything and could never be surprised. Even I, who didn't know everything, found it almost impossible to pay attention for more than a few seconds at a time to anything anybody else had to say, to abandon the conversation that was perpetually going on inside my head and enter into those of other people—

ones filled with pauses and reconsiderations, contradictions and asides, repetitions and explanations of things so simple they would bore a child. Even at readings and performances and plays where I had gone specifically to immerse myself in somebody else's consciousness I could do no more than sample bits and pieces of what I had paid money to see and hear: I would try, but lists of errands, phone calls, bodily discomforts, and old arguments would play and replay themselves in my mind.

There was one significant exception to this: when I wanted to go to bed with someone. Then I listened, but what I was really listening to was the conversation underneath the ostensible conversation, the one that went: I find you physically attractive enough to want to have sex with you, do you find me physically attractive enough to want to have sex with me?

I asked God to forgive me for being such a scumbag. Then I asked God to forgive my presumption in presuming that He (I had trouble thinking of God as a She) was bored: God, being all-powerful, could decree that God not be bored.

Despite the garden, nobody seemed to be coming to this bar, so I walked back to the one where I had been the previous two nights. The woman from Pantry Pride was there; she insisted on buying me a beer. I drank some of it with her, then excused myself to go to the ladies room. I wouldn't have bothered if it wasn't necessary to escape from her, but once there I decided I really did have to pee. Is it possible to be near a toilet and not have to use it? I wasn't sure whether the door was to a room that had several booths in it, or whether the door was the door to the bathroom itself, so I waited for someone to come out. When the door opened, I saw a group of people standing inside by the sink, talking and smoking. Although it was a ladies' room men were in there as well as women, which made me feel comfortable enough to walk inside: if men were there I couldn't be accused of entering the bathroom so I could make a pass at a woman. As I waited for a stall one of the men passed a joint to me, and I took a hit. It seemed less conspicuous than not taking one, then I took another, so people wouldn't think I was smoking just out of politeness, but because I was the kind of person who really liked drugs. I tried to pass the joint on, but nobody wanted it, and I had to continue holding onto it and smoking it. Surreptitiously I tried to exhale so I wouldn't get too high.

When I got inside the stall I unrolled a huge wad of toilet paper which I held under me as I peed, so nobody could hear my urine dropping into the toilet. But the paper began to disintegrate as soon as it got wet and some of the urine got on my hand. I had to unroll more paper to wipe off my hand, and then it occurred to me that perhaps people had been listening to this double unrolling of the toilet paper, and that if they put their minds to it they could figure out what I had been doing. I realized this was worse than if they had just heard me peeing.

I told myself this kind of thinking had to do with the marijuana. I forced myself to zip up my pants and leave the toilet. Carefully I washed my hands to get off the urine. I looked at myself in the mirror. I was pleased with what I saw. The heat in the bar had made the ends of my hair slightly damp, so that I looked something like an Italian movie star who's just climbed out of the Mediterranean to get back on a yacht. The joint came my way again, and again I took it. "There's hash in there," someone said. That was okay, I said, I liked hash. I looked at my face again and laughed, then I left the bathroom and went to the dance floor. I didn't take the direct route through the downstairs bar where the girl from Pantry Pride was, but the other, more circuitous one—up the stairs to the rooftop bar, then across that bar and down another set of stairs.

A man and woman were dancing. His shirt was off, exposing a lean but muscular, almost hairless chest. He held a scarf in his hands that he swirled in a way that fit the movements of his body so well that although it was incredibly sexy it was also somehow totally pure, and the woman was dancing with him so that the movements of her body fit him and his scarf as if they had been dancing together like this for years; they were so absolutely right that almost the whole room had stopped to watch them. And yet there was nothing virtuosic about what they were doing, they really seemed to be doing it for themselves, so that instead of resenting them you had to join in their pleasure. They were as perfect together as two people dancing can be, though of the two, he was more perfect. He was at least sixty. She was in her twenties, with freckles. Even as they danced I kept worrying about it ending, how they would handle the transition to another song. As much as I wanted to continue watching them I knew esthetically it was right for them to stop; whatever they did after this could only be anticlimactic. These two desires—the desire for them to stop and the desire for them to continue— seemed both contradictory and emblematic, and I realized that this rather middle-aged principle—abstinence in the service of voluptuousness—could perhaps be extended to other pleasures as well.

The song ended. The man picked up the shirt he had discarded and flung it unbuttoned around his shoulders. Other people began to drift back on the floor. "Terrific," I told him. He smiled. For once I was not self-conscious; I had forgotten myself in the magic of the moment. But it was the girl I really wanted, the blond girl with the

enormous blue eyes who probably did not own a house by
the ocean. Still, I would consent to share my life with her.

She was walking away. Any second my self-consciousness
would return. I ran up to her and touched her on the
shoulder. She turned towards me. "You're the most attractive person in Key West," I said, meaning, of course,
the world. She laughed, then joined her friends. She must
have told them what I said, for they giggled as they looked
at me. I waved at them, then walked over and introduced
myself. Cherry told me her name, and I bought us both a
beer. To show me the beer didn't mean I owned her, she
left me to go talk to some other people. I could tell it
would be a mistake to follow her, so I stayed with her
friends. I knew she would be back.

You know these kinds of girls; they're waitresses, sell
T-shirts or cheap jewelry, lead tours on the miniature
train. When they're young they're beautiful, or at least
attractive, then all of a sudden it's gone. Remembering
this, you think you made a mistake, the mistake of infat-
uation—but no, if you look, the photograph is just right;
they *were* beautiful, but with the kind of beauty that dies.
They talked the way I expected them to: who did or didn't
call whom, what parties they were going to over the
weekend, new kinds of makeup, clothing sales. If this had
been New York they would have had a Queens accent and
I would have despised them. But I tried to get them to
like me for Cherry's sake. For a while they let me listen to
them, then they began to ask me questions about myself.

"Still here?" Cherry said, when she rejoined us.

"Of course. How could I leave the most beautiful girl
in Key West?"

"Watch it, Cherry, she's a tricky one."

"Tricky? Who could be more open than me?"

"She said she's a famous writer," said one of her friends.

"But we've never heard of her," laughed another.

"Famous in my family," I said.

"Yeah, I'm famous in my family too!"

"We could go to a bookstore and look for my book," I offered.

Of course they didn't move. I didn't expect them to. Luckily. My novel—at that time I had published only one—almost certainly wouldn't be on the shelves of a bookstore in Key West; it was no longer in bookstores in New York City.

"She doesn't look like a writer."

"Writers don't wear shirts like that."

"Listen to what she said: 'Who could be more famous than *me*?' "

"I have editors to check up on my grammar. That's what editors are for," I explained.

"Oh yeah, then I can write a novel too."

"*Hot Nights in Miami.*"

"*Two Thousand and One Margaritas.*"

"*My Cheating Heart*, a.k.a. *Cherry's Crazy Husband.*"

"Cherry's married?" I asked. They laughed hysterically. "You're not married?" I asked her. We had barely spoken, except through friends.

"Don't listen to them. They're idiots."

"Will you spend the night with me?"

"Maybe." She gave me a huge smile. "Then again, maybe I won't."

I loved this. "I could fall in love with you," I told her.

"You're crazy! Did you hear what she said?" she told her friends. "She could fall in love with me!" But you could see she liked it.

They insisted on going someplace else. One of them needed a hamburger, or maybe it was a pizza. We stuffed ourselves into one car and drove to the strip, ending up at an ugly place with prefabricated paneling, the kind you find off highways in New Jersey. On the way back Cherry sat on my lap. I ran my hand up the back of her blouse. I could feel the straps of her bra through the cloth. I wondered what it would be like to live here with her, to go to barbecues and talk about haircuts and who didn't call who for the next ten years. Just how far would I go for a pretty face?

I told myself it would be far, very far, much farther than anyone I knew. The idea of being with someone stupid and unworthy—but with a heartbreaking, sexy beauty everybody would covet—exerted a powerful hold on my imagination. It seemed the wittiest and nerviest thing I could do; I yearned to boast about it, years later, in a bar. It was why my friends called me romantic, or immature. But I worried whether, when the great moment came, I'd have the guts to live up to my choice.

Meanwhile Cherry's friends were talking about couples who were breaking up, gay motels in Miami, cocaine.

We had just finished negotiating the logistics for us spending the night together when a friend of hers suggested that, since Cherry didn't know me from Adam and for all they knew I might be a dangerous psychopath, they look for my book in a bookstore to see if I was really a writer. "She can buy you a copy," one of them said. "After all, if you go home with her, the least she can do is give you a free book."

"If it gets really boring, at least I'll have something to do!" she joked.

"Wow! I didn't know they taught people in the south how to read!" I replied.

In resort towns stores stay open late. My novel wasn't

there. I asked the manager if I could look at *Books in Print*. It wasn't listed there either.

"You see, she's a liar."

"I'm not a liar. My book is out of print."

"Yeah. Right. I'm a Hollywood actress, just not in any movie. Ha ha ha."

By the time we'd returned to the original bar, Cherry's friends had persuaded her not to go home with me. Most writers I know carry copies of their books with them when they go on vacations, and I cursed my peculiar lack of vanity in leaving mine at home, which in my heart I felt was vanity in some other guise. I did not want to think of myself as someone who needed a prop. I decided to go back to my hotel. Like many grownup tourists in Key West, I had rented a bike to get around town with, but I felt like an idiot unlocking it in front of them. I could just imagine the jokes they were making about the famous writer riding a bike.

Often I had not gotten what I wanted, but never before had something I'd been promised been ripped out of my grasp. The injustice of it infuriated me. I *was* a writer, I *wasn't* lying. I wanted to phone up somebody to complain about it, but the only person I could call up at that hour was my girlfriend. I had a slight fever from my sunburn. All in all, I barely slept.

The next day I looked through the yellow pages and found the location of every bookstore in Key West. None of them had my book; none of them had old copies of *Books in Print*. I tried the local and the college library; also no luck. Finally I called my girlfriend and told her she had to Fed Ex my novel to me. I told her I had met a producer who was crazy to see my book, but he was going back to L.A. in a few days.

"Why don't you wait and send him the novel in L.A.?" she asked.

"You know producers."

She thought it was stupid, but finally agreed. I told myself I should have felt guilty but I didn't. Did my girlfriend feel guilty when she coerced me into having sex with her, even though she must have known I didn't love her?

That night I looked for Cherry in the bar where we had met. After two hours I tried the other bar, but she wasn't there either. I had my fourth beer and knew I couldn't hold out much longer, but I went back to the first bar. I was desperate and pathetic and hated myself. Even if I had run into Cherry, there was no way I could have convinced her to spend the night with me. The best thing was for me not to run into her; nonetheless, it was past one before I gave up and went back to my hotel.

The next day I kept asking the man at the hotel whether a package had arrived for me.

It was the custom in Key West for tourists to gather on the pier to watch the sun set. Although there was no reason on earth for her to be there, I walked through the crowds looking for Cherry. Except for me, everybody seemed to be in groups or couples: men and women, women and women, men and men. Looking at them made me sick. Why was I alone in front of an orange-and-purple sky? Why was I ever alone under any color sky? I completely forgot I had a girlfriend. Why had I made that stupid suggestion about looking for my book in the bookstore? Why couldn't I remember where Cherry worked? I decided to go to the bar early for a change. Maybe she and her friends met there for happy hour after work.

I sat with my beer at the bar staring at the door. Already many of the customers looked familiar. A few of the men nodded at me. Neither Cherry nor her friends appeared, and after an hour I dragged myself off to dinner. My loneliness seemed immutable, iconographic, inevitable.

I ate my rock shrimp alone. I was depressed and told myself to go back to the hotel, but again I found myself at the bar. "Dark Heineken's?" the bartender asked, remembering my preference. I felt embarrassed, as if I were an alcoholic. To prove I wasn't, I ordered a Perrier with lime. Then I realized this might make it look like I was trying to go on the wagon, so I changed my mind and told him to give me the beer after all.

I couldn't sit still, so I went to the other bar. I played pinball for a while, then went out to the garden. As usual the place was quite empty. Perhaps it was a front for laundering money. I tried to think about my new novel, the one I was supposed to start after coming back from this trip, but my mind just kept repeating: Cherry, Cherry, Cherry. It was a weird, salacious name. I told myself that if only she had slept with me the first night none of this would have happened: I would probably be on the plane right now, going home to my girlfriend. It was no consolation.

I couldn't help myself, I went back to the other bar. It was like a nightmare where there's a train you have to catch, only there's stuff you keep forgetting to pack and by the time you arrive the train is pulling out of the station. Cherry wasn't there, but I saw the woman from Pantry Pride. Another beer would make me totally drunk, but I let her buy me one—the price I extracted for the privilege of coming home with me. I was not in a sexual mood, but I thought it would be good for my ego.

Usually I know everything, but this was one of those times I was wrong. I was dry and distracted and kept praying for her to stop.

"Is something the matter?" she eventually asked.

I couldn't help myself, I asked her if she knew a girl named Cherry: blond hair, freckled, with big blue eyes.

"Oh yeah, she's a bitch."

"What do you mean?"

"Her friends think they're such hot shit." With some prodding, she told me Cherry sold tickets for one of the glass-bottom boats.

"Do you really have a child?" I asked.

"Yes. She's six."

"Six! How old are you?"

"Twenty-eight."

"God, you look younger. How can you go out so often?"

"We live with my mother."

She took my hand and put it inside her. She was extremely wet, and it disgusted me.

When I came down for breakfast the next morning the clerk told me my package had arrived. I took a manila envelope, a pad and pen, and my novel, and biked down toward the pier. There were a number of glass-bottom boats docked there, each with its own ticket booth. I walked past them looking for Cherry. When I didn't see her, I asked the girls selling tickets if a blond girl with that name worked there.

When I found the right place, I opened my book and wrote on the title page: "To the most attractive woman in Key West—from someone who's not a liar." I also left a note: "Miss you like crazy. Meet you-know-where tonight at 11." I signed it: "The Writer." I put her name on the outside of the envelope, sealed it, then I headed for the beach.

"You're crazy," Cherry said at eleven that night when she joined me. But there was a big smile on her face.

"That's what you told me the night I met you."

"I started reading your book. I really like it. I think it's very good." I waited for her to tell me in which ways she thought it good, but she didn't say anything.

"What exactly do you like?" I prodded her.

"Oh, the characters and everything. It's very funny."

"How far have you gotten?"

"Well. Not all that far."

"How far?"

"Seven or eight pages."

One of her friends was with her. "That's more than she's read in the last two years." They laughed. Across the room, I saw the woman from Pantry Pride looking at me. I knew that in the hierarchy of Key West she wasn't the equal of Cherry's friends, so I pretended not to see her.

I was with Cherry, at last, in my room. I moved towards her to embrace her, but immediately she began throwing off her clothes. It seemed somewhat cold and businesslike, but I sat down on the edge of the bed and took off my shoes. I stopped to watch her. She was whiter in the moonlight, her freckles invisible. She plopped herself down on the bed as if I weren't there. Self-consciously I finished taking off my clothes and lay down next to her. We had not yet kissed.

When we did, I had trouble concentrating. The previous night I had had trouble being with the woman from Pantry Pride because I was thinking of Cherry, and now I had trouble being with Cherry because I was thinking of Cherry—not the one in my bed but the one in my head. I couldn't get over the fact she was really here with me. I kept thinking about the past few days, how I'd walked back and forth from bar to bar searching for her, how I had made my girlfriend send me my book, how if Cherry knew all the trouble I'd gone to to be with her she probably wouldn't want to be with me. On the surface I felt phenomenally lucky to be with her, but on another level I felt the opposite, that she was phenomenally lucky to be with me. You would have thought these contradictory beliefs would have evened themselves out—by my thinking each of us phenomenally lucky to be with the other—but oddly I didn't feel that way at all.

Our kissing wasn't occupying my mind sufficiently. I think it wasn't active enough for all I had gone through. It seemed we should have gone swimming first, raced bikes, at least danced, so I could have gotten tired enough to fall into my trance. She was so perfect she intimidated me; my presence seemed to destroy her perfection. On some level I felt I was beautiful, but it was not the obvious level, and I didn't trust her to appreciate this.

My girlfriend often told me I was beautiful, but this only increased my contempt for her.

In search of my trance I slid down Cherry's body.

Normally I start out with a slow and steady rhythm which very gradually (so as to avoid any suggestion of rush—for what destroys orgasm faster than anxiety?) intensifies via both increased speed and pressure of my tongue so as to create a sense of progression and destination in my partner, occasionally interrupted by rather randomly placed deviations from this progression in order to suggest unpredictability and uncertainty, hence poignancy. But for some reason this night I found myself altering my rhythms arbitrarily, without coherence or intelligible pattern to my movements, realizing I'd stopped doing something successful only when it was too late. I tried to match my breathing to her breathing so she'd know I knew how she was feeling (although I did not), which usually leads to feelings of trust, togetherness, and increased excitement—but this was hard because the noises she was making sounded false to me and it was hard to mimic them sincerely.

"Wait a sec," she said, suddenly pushing me away. She got off the bed and went down on her knees on the floor. I wondered if this were some odd sexual perversion I was supposed to participate in. Perhaps she was pretending to be a dog. Did she want me to put a belt around her neck and pretend it was a collar and lead her around? Or did she just want to make love on the floor? She was patting the ground, sort of like cats do after they shit. I bent down and kissed the back of her neck, then reached for her breast.

She evaded my hand. "I lost my earring," she explained.

"Oh. Why don't we look for it later?"

"I'm afraid I'll forget about it."

"I won't. I've got a great memory."

She turned on the light, but we couldn't find the earring. "Maybe it fell off in the car," I suggested.

"I don't think so. I'm sure I had it when I came in here."

When she went into the bathroom, I turned off the light. I was irritated at her about the earring, and irritated at myself for not being able to make love to her properly. Why were my mind and body so far apart? She got back in bed with me, but after a few more minutes she got up again. She began putting on her blouse.

"You're not leaving?" I asked.

"Yeah, I gotta go." She looked at her watch.

"Let's have dinner tomorrow," I suggested. She was silent. "My treat," I added.

"I don't know. I think I'm busy."

"Give me your number, I'll call you."

"I'll be at work."

"I'll stop by. What time are you there?"

"I'm not sure. It varies. That's not a good idea anyway."

"Look, if you want to meet me for dinner, leave a message at the hotel. Or I'll look for you later at the bar."

We kissed goodbye in a perfunctory fashion. I did not have the guts to ask her if I should have done something else, like slap her.

I lay in bed after she had gone, wondering what had gone wrong. I thought of my girlfriend, then of the woman from Pantry Pride. A deep dissatisfaction flowed through me. It had been there all my life. Even when I got what I wanted, it was no good; somewhere deep inside I felt compelled to destroy it.

The next morning when I called my girlfriend to tell her I would be away a few more days, she asked me what the producer had thought of the book. I almost said "*what producer?*" but I caught myself in time.

■ ■ ■

I drove myself crazy looking for Cherry's earring, not just in my room but around the hotel, but I couldn't find it. I decided to buy her a pair. I walked up and down the rows of hippie booths for over an hour, eventually narrowing my choice to an amusing set of dangling pineapples, or a more expensive and serious pair of silver and turquoise. Unable to decide, I bought both. I would consider the decision further over lunch, and keep the pair I didn't give her for myself.

My impulse was to give her the expensive ones, but I thought she might think I was a jerk—as I would have if the woman from Pantry Pride had bought something expensive for me. On the other hand, depending on her level of sophistication, she might think the pineapples tacky instead of amusing. Ultimately I decided neither was acceptable, so I bought a third set, esthetically similar to the silver and turquoise pair but not quite so pretty—or expensive. I brought them to where Cherry worked. She wasn't there, so I left them with a note saying I'd be at the bar around eleven.

A little past the time I'd told Cherry to meet me, her friend—the one who'd suggested we go to the bookstore— tapped me on the shoulder. She handed me a paper bag. Inside it were the earrings I had bought Cherry that day.

"What's the matter?" I asked.

"Are you stupid or what? She doesn't want to see you anymore."

"That's impossible. She just slept with me!"

She looked at me like I was an idiot. "You better not

leave her any more messages," she warned. "This isn't New York, you know. She could lose her job."

I put the earrings in my pocket and finished my beer, then I walked over to the other bar. I felt sick, in shock, unbelieving. A number of women were there, attractive women I might have liked if I had not seen Cherry first. I sat there a while listening to the cicadas in the garden, then I went back to my hotel.

Early the next day I went down to the pier off which people like me swam. In my pursuit of bookstores, ticket booths, and earrings, I'd been neglecting my tan. I let myself get very hot, then I went into the water. I decided to swim for a long long time, until I became so exhausted that the sorrows of my life no longer had the power to affect me. What was my life that I should care about it so much? It was just a drop in the streams of time. At first I was conscious of the salt, the other swimmers, the possible presence of barracuda, but gradually the rhythm of my arms took over, and I forgot everything but the movements of my hands in and out of the water, the rise and fall of the waves and the sun on my back, I was in that state where you feel you can swim forever. I had left my goggles on the beach, perhaps so as to torture myself even further; soon the salt was stinging my eyes so badly I had to keep them closed. This didn't bother me, it only added to my trance. The trance, oddly, did not remove me from the present, but connected me more closely to it, so that each second was completely whole and interesting in itself, yet in an odd way I also felt detached, as if I had no stake in what was happening. I felt I could have responded with total honesty, total lack of self-consciousness, to any ques-

tion anyone asked, and done what I wanted with total
spontaneity, without caring what anyone thought. Sensations were everything; desires were nothing. We associated
desire with sensation but that was a mistake; desire was a
yearning for sensation, the craving for what was not there
rather than for what was there. Sometimes desire was so
intense that it created sensation, simply out of the power
of my imagination—my pants getting wet without anyone
even touching me; other times its intensity destroyed
sensation, as it had the other night with Cherry. I used
"romance" to create meaning around sexual acts so that
their sensations would be intensified, but the necessity of
romance so greatly limited the possible agents of sensation
that the likelihood of my experiencing the sensations I
supposedly craved was very small. When my sensations in
bed with someone were extremely intense I had a fear we
would stay there forever until we died; was desire, for me,
a way of preventing sensation, so that I could continue to
live, write, maintain a body that would continue having
thoughts like this? My desires, at this moment, seemed
unimportant, petty. If I desired sensation, wouldn't it be
most efficient to respond to the person nearest at hand—
the person who wanted me? Wasn't that what a saint—
or God—would do, instead of caring about the color of
someone's hair or eyes, or whether they were a few pounds
overweight? Of course that should also mean that the
person I wanted should respond to me too, simply because
I wanted them, but it was up to someone to start acting
the proper way, and—according to the categorical imper-
ative and because the idea had occurred to me first—that
person logically should be me. Out in the ocean, where
there was no Cherry but only sun and salt and water—
sun that stung my back as salt stung my eyes, the water

easing the stings even as being in it created them—where I felt happiness in the way of fish, this seemed totally possible, and I had a vision of a sane and happy life in which everybody satisfied everybody else, and nobody's wants went unfulfilled. It seemed possible, as swimming to Cuba seemed possible, and yet I knew it was not possible, though I also told myself it was only my own mind that was telling me it was not possible. If my mind told me it was possible it would come true. Of course it was totally possible I did not want sanity and happiness. My hand struck something. In panic I opened my eyes. It was not a barracuda, it was the dock.

Late in the afternoon I went to where Cherry worked. I was feeling good because of my swim and confident she would like me when she saw how relaxed and unselfconscious I was. My only worry was that she would not be there to see me at my best, but she was. "Leave me alone. I don't want anything to do with you," she told me as soon as I reached the booth.

"I don't understand. What happened? All I want is to see you again. Not necessarily to have sex—just to talk."

She looked up. A man from the boat was approaching. "Please go away. You're gonna get me fired."

"Only if you'll agree to meet me. Eight o'clock at the bar?"

"All right. Just get out of here."

I waited at the bar until nine-thirty, trying to tell myself she was coming, but not really believing this. But I also couldn't believe she didn't want to see me again. I wasn't a ditzbrain like her and her friends, I was a writer from New York who was willing to spend the rest of my life with a ditzbrain like her.

Between the swimming and the waiting, I was famished. I quickly ate a slice of pizza from the stand across the street, then I came back to the bar. Someone had taken my seat. I felt the guy at the door and the bartender and the waiters were all staring at me. I compared the conspicuousness I had felt the first night in this bar to the conspicuousness I was feeling now, and realized how much worse this new kind was. At ten-thirty, I left for the other bar.

Cherry was in the garden with her friends. When she saw me she turned her back on me.

I could not help myself, I walked over.

"Cherry," I said, a beer in my hand.

"Ignore her," she said to the person next to her, a big, dark-haired butch type I hadn't seen her with before. "She's out of her mind."

"You promised to meet me. I don't understand. It's not fair."

She stood up and walked away. Her friends followed her. I started to walk after them but someone grabbed my arm. It was the butch-looking woman. She was much stronger than me. "Leave her alone."

"I just want to talk to her."

"Keep bothering her and your pretty little face won't be so pretty anymore." This was *film noir* language, and I laughed. "You think it's funny?" she said, gripping my arm tighter. "Wait and see how funny it is."

"I was laughing at the way you were talking, not at what

you were saying." She looked like she wanted to punch me. I think I wanted her to.

"You're a sick fuck," she said.

"Look, are you her lover?" I asked. "I'm not trying to come between you. I just want to talk to her." I turned to Cherry. "Will you please come and talk to me? Just for a few minutes. Over there if you want, in full view of your friends, if you're so frightened of me."

"Let's get out of here," Cherry told her friend.

"Five minutes, that's all. *Five* fucking minutes!"

"Come on," said Cherry. "She's crazy." Her friend dropped my arm and followed her out of the bar.

"Crazy! Why the fuck did you sleep with me then, you fucking cunt?" I shouted after them.

Across the garden people were looking at me as if *I* were the one who was crazy, as if I were the only one who had ever been treated this way, as if, unlike me, they had never been betrayed.

I followed them to the other bar, but when they saw me they got into their car. From across the street I watched the taillights disappear around the corner. My blue-eyed, freckled piece of southern trash—I would never have a chance to boast in a bar how I had thrown away my life for her.

"You can't come in here like that," the guy at the door stopped me. I felt panicked, as you do in the night when you wake up and realize you haven't been breathing. Was the owner of the bar a friend of Cherry's lover? Had the other bar called to warn them about me? Had they decided I was just too much of a jerk?

It turned out the problem was the beer I was still carrying from the other bar. I left it in the gutter and went inside.

The woman from Pantry Pride was there. She walked away when she saw me, but I followed her upstairs to the rooftop bar. "I'm leaving tomorrow," I told her. "Don't hold a grudge." She said she didn't want a beer, but I ordered two anyway. "I'm sorry," I said. "This woman Cherry really did a number on me."

"You're a real bitch," she said. "You know?"

"I know." Then I remembered my swim in the water, the ways in which I was also a saint. "You know, I'm really not."

"No. *You really are!*" We chugged our beers in silence. When she was done I stood up.

"I'm exhausted, I gotta split. You gonna spend the night with me or what?"

"Why the fuck should I?"

"Because you've got this thing about me," I said. "Let's go."

A half hour later I was on my bed, my legs spread wide, every nerve of my body on fire. It was sensation, but not desire.

"It wouldn't exactly kill you to touch me," she said. I remembered I was a saint, so I tried. "Like you mean it, huh?"

She cried out in pleasure, though as usual it sounded like pain.

the duchess of l.a.

My friend Linda used to be an ordinary housewife married to a professor in Westwood, but she had artistic aspirations, and when she and her husband split up she began to hang around with a hip L.A. crowd, people who went to poetry readings, art openings, clubs. She met a poet named Jack who moved in with her and her cats and her two kids. Jack was nice and a good poet, but sexually he had his quirks. He had been immobilized in a full body cast for six months because of a car accident in his childhood, and the memory of that bondage held him in thrall. He liked—"needed" is perhaps a better word—to be tied up, spanked, suspended, insulted. Although Linda had begun to make assemblages, she was still pretty much the same nice Jewish housewife she had always been, and she tried to oblige him. Paddles, collars, handcuffs and restraints of various kinds, even a cage for Jack to sleep in, soon made their appearance in the Westwood house. Some of it she kept locked up in a little room where Jack had his desk, but the cage was too large to hide from her children. Her daughter began to spend nights at her father's house; her son quit the high school soccer team and began to indulge in the standard drugs. For brief moments Linda would be very upset about this, then she would dismiss it as one of those things you grow out of in time. One time the fetish closet was broken into, and after that pee began to appear in the morning all over the son's bathroom, which was also the guest bathroom. Her son said it was because if he turned on the light to pee he couldn't get back to sleep; Jack told her it was because of the fetish objects. I kept wondering when Linda would cut it out and find a nice lawyer to marry and take care of the mortgage payments, but one year passed, then another, and Jack was still there.

It is impossible to know human beings. You think you know them and most of the time you do, but then they will do something to surprise you and you can't fit this in with anything else you know about them, and the fact that you have been able to predict with near certainty their actions in the past only adds to this puzzlement. But I still felt like I really knew Linda, that she was only pretending to be this other person and any day would revert back to the one I knew. I was supposed to be the hip person in our relationship, and this change irritated me. Thus, although when I was with her I pretended to admire her new life, I didn't. I had enough friends who wrote, painted, danced, sung; I had been glad to have a friend who was basically just a nice Jewish girl. She now said things like she couldn't feel complete unless she could build objects that expressed the things that had been hidden inside her for years. I suppose everyone has stuff hidden inside them, but the world would be even more cluttered if everyone felt like they had to convert it into bits of metal, wood, and plastic. Nonetheless, I was in the habit of being her friend, and I saw her and Jack whenever they came to New York.

One time I was in L.A., and I stayed for a few days in her house. The son was still peeing all over the bathroom; Linda warned me to be sure to wipe off the toilet seat before sitting on it. Or maybe I should just squat over it, the way you did in Africa or Asia. At night we went to punk clubs where people looked like people had in New York a year or two before—but more so.

"What happened to your furniture?" I asked. We were sitting on cushions in her livingroom, just as if it were 1968.

"It's kind of a long story . . ." said Linda. She looked at Jack.

"Just tell her the truth," said Jack. "It was our night for the club, and things got a little out of hand."

"What club?"

"Oh, just a club that meets sometimes at our house."

"What kind of club destroys the furniture?"

It turned out to be a kind of liberation organization to protect the rights of people to beat, bind, give enemas to, and urinate on each other, as well as perform other similar such acts. Although the focus of the meeting was usually on theory rather than *praxis*, sometimes things got out of hand. Linda was the chairwoman.

"You're kidding!" To my knowledge, Linda had never run anything bigger than a yard sale.

"Jewish women," said Jack. "They're used to ordering people around."

"Yeah. Everybody wants to be a slave but me." She sighed.

During my stay Linda and Jack had a lot of squabbles. Most of these seemed to revolve around Jack wanting Linda to order him to do things, and Linda refusing to do this. "You're crazy," I told her. "Why don't you make him go shopping and clean up the house? Do the laundry. Wipe up the pee in the bathroom. Give you a massage. Or won't he do stuff like that?"

"He'll do anything I tell him," she assured me smugly. "We have a three-month contract."

"What does that mean?"

"He has to do whatever I want for three months, and if he doesn't I have the right to punish him."

"If I were you I'd take advantage of it. You're always telling me how you can't stand housework."

"I know. But it's not that simple."

"So you lock him up in the dog cage at night to make him happy. So what?"

"I can't explain it," she said. "It's very complicated. You really should read this thing I wrote." She went to her desk and pulled out some xeroxed sheets that were stapled together. So Linda had become a philosopher. That night we went over to the house of a woman who was Linda's main slave. She was skinny and pale, as if she hadn't been in the sun in years, and it was obvious Jack was jealous of her. After dinner Judy cleared up and then Linda told her to go into the bedroom and get things ready.

"Can I join you?" asked Jack.

"No. But if you want, you can kneel outside the door on your knees and listen to us."

"On my hands and knees or just my knees?"

"On your hands and knees. Don't move. Be sure to tell me if he moves," she said to me. "He'll be punished very severely if he does."

"How?" I asked.

"I'll probably tie him up outside the house all night with a gag in his mouth. It's supposed to rain and he'll catch a cold. Jack hates colds."

"Nobody likes colds," said Jack.

Linda got up to leave the room, then stopped. "If you'd like, you could come inside and watch us," she told me. "It would give you a better sense of what I'm into."

"Judy wouldn't mind?"

Linda gave me a somewhat patronizing smile. "It doesn't matter. After all, she's my slave."

I wasn't really interested in what they were doing, but I felt Linda would be insulted if I told her that, so after a few moments of watching Jack kneel like a dog, I followed her into the bedroom.

Judy was dressed only in her underpants. A number of objects, some of which I had never seen before, were lying on the bed: a whip, hand restraints, a paddle, several metal devices that looked like those things we held the remnants of joints with in the late sixties, short chains with pieces of lead on the ends. Linda told Judy she was going to perform something called "breastwork" on her. She took the things that looked like roach clips and put one on each breast. "Ow," said Judy. Linda pulled on these a bit and asked Judy how she liked it. "It hurts," said Judy. Linda nodded and with much seriousness told her that was good. Then she took several of the lead pieces and attached the chains to the roach clips. "Ow," Judy said again. Then Linda told Judy to take off her pants. Judy stepped out of the pants and laid herself across Linda's lap. Linda picked up the paddle and began to spank her. But for some reason she wasn't pleased with this and told Judy to get the hairbrush that was lying on the bureau. Linda explained to me how you couldn't use your hand to spank someone because it hurt too much—not the person you're spanking but your hand. The spanking was done in a slow and rather desultory fashion, as if Linda were performing a somewhat tedious but necessary task. Occasionally I peeked out the door at Jack. As commanded, he was kneeling like a dog on all fours. It was hard to sense the connection between these acts and sex, though I don't know exactly what else you could call it.

When the spanking was done, Linda told Judy to put on a pair of latex panties. They were a hideous thick green rubber. Linda told me the point of them was to keep Judy's ass hot, in order to prolong the pain and memory of the spanking after Linda was gone. Then she asked Judy to please make some coffee for herself and me.

"What would you like in it?" Judy asked.

"Just bring everything in on a tray. I think we'd better have some milk, and cream, and sugar—or maybe honey, if you'd prefer that?" she asked me.

"Sure."

"And some cinnamon. Please use the silver tray. And cloth napkins, please. Not paper."

When Judy opened the door we could see Jack still kneeling there. Jack asked Linda if he could come into the room and join us. She told him no, he had to stay in this position until we left the house, but she said we would keep the door open so he could hear what we were saying.

He could listen, but he was not allowed to say anything himself until we were in the car.

Judy brought in the coffee as ordered. She had added some cookies on her own initiative and Linda reprimanded her for this, saying she should have asked permission first. But I told Linda I was in the mood for cookies, so Linda decided not to punish her after all. Meanwhile, as Linda and I sat on the bed eating and drinking and talking about Judy and Jack, Judy sat in her green latex panties at the foot of the bed. At first I felt self-conscious, but I quickly grew to like it. There was something very leisurely about it all, as if I were a pasha. Soon Judy and Jack became invisible. Oddly, this did not make it harder to be with them later, but easier.

Before we left, Judy asked Linda if she could go to the bathroom.

Linda looked at her watch. "No."

"Please. I have to."

"Judy, you asked me and I said no. I don't like to be questioned when I tell you something."

"I'm sorry."

"That's better."

"When am I going to be allowed to go?"

"I'm not sure."

"But I have to go." One leg rubbed against the other.

"Judy, this is very bad." Linda shook her head sadly. "We're going to leave now. In one hour you may call and ask my permission to go to the bathroom. I may pick up my phone or I may have my machine on, I don't know."

"Couldn't she cheat?" I asked Linda in the car.

"What would be the point of that?"

Jack began to explain poopoo sex to me. Sometimes you wouldn't let someone go when they had to, and sometimes you made them go even if they didn't want to, by giving them an enema. After administering the enema, you would forbid them to go—which of course they would be unable not to do—then you would punish them when they did.

This seemed even less like sex than Jack's kneeling outside the door. "Do you do that a lot?" I asked, in the same tone I would ask them if they had seen the latest Bertolucci film.

"Not much," said Linda. "We have enough bathroom problems with my son."

Linda asked me if I had read her article and what I had thought about it. I said it was interesting but a little murky, as if she had been reading too much semiotics. She rolled her eyes at Jack as if I were some philistine.

"Have you heard of Duchess La Jeanne?" Jack asked me.

"No."

"Well, that's Linda's public name. She's the most famous dominatrix in L.A."

That night, despite Jack's docility in kneeling outside Judy's bedroom, he was forced to sleep outside in the dog cage. There was a kind of wall covered by ivy around the property, but there was nothing to prevent a neighbor from peeking through and seeing this, let alone Linda's son. I realized that in peeing all over the bathroom he was not just expressing his displeasure, he was acting like a *dog*. It did rain, and Jack was sniffling the next day. By the time I left for New York a few days later, it had turned into a mild form of pneumonia.

"They say people don't die for love," joked Jack. "But maybe they do."

"I nearly died once of a broken heart," I said. "But I guess that's only a metaphor."

"I take love seriously, but sometimes I wonder if it matters that much who I'm with," said Linda. "Like if Jack died, as horrible as this sounds, I'm sure I'd soon be in love with someone else."

Jack did not seem shocked by this, but I was. Not just that she had said it, but that she had thought it. It was the kind of thing I could imagine myself thinking, though probably not saying, but Linda?

"I often think I don't like people, but when they leave I miss them," I said.

"I never missed my husband when he left," said Linda.

Jack told us about a boy in high school he had had a tremendous crush on. He still regretted not having sex with him, even though he had never slept with a man and had no interest in doing so. He didn't like the idea of having to do stuff with a man's asshole; that was one of the reasons he wasn't into enemas. But women were a different matter. He thought it was a very sexy thing to watch women make love together. That was why he had encouraged Linda and Judy, only it had backfired against him because they never let him join in.

"That doesn't seem fair," I said.

"I think I'll renegotiate it in the next contract," said Jack.

"I don't know about any more contracts," said Linda.

"Is something the matter between you guys?" I asked her the next night. We were driving to The Marquis d'O, a sex club that had a woman's night once a month.

Sometimes it was good and lots of sexy people turned up, sometimes it was terrible.

"Well . . . I don't know. In a way I think this relationship has run its course."

"You're not in love with Judy?" I asked.

"Maybe," said Linda. "Sometimes I think I am. She needs me so much."

I thought of mentioning that her children, who needed her too, did not seem to receive much of the benefits of Linda's empathy. "What about Jack? He seems to need you too."

"I know," she sighed. "That's the problem." She paused. "Jack'll be okay. I'll always be there for him. He knows that."

"Are you really the most famous dominatrix in L.A.?" I asked.

"Yes. It's a great way for people like us to make money and not have it interfere with their art. You make a hundred dollars an hour, sometimes more—not including tips."

"What do you have to do?"

"Insults, dressing up, enemas, spankings. You negotiate with the customer. If it's something really disgusting, I won't do it."

"I can't believe it, Linda," I said. "I still think of you as a nice Jewish girl."

"I *am* a nice Jewish girl. Don't you think you're a little naïve?" We pulled into the parking place.

"Tsk," Linda said, that sound of the tongue between the teeth. Only ten or twelve women were in the club, which smelled of old liquor and cigarettes. A fat woman dressed in a black leather slip and halter stood behind the bar. She gave Linda and me free drinks. Everyone seemed to know Linda. The women were incredibly unattractive, overweight or unduly skinny, with pale unhealthy-looking skin—unless this was due to the lighting, which seemed designed to make everyone look like heroin addicts. They were dressed in predictable ways: black leather pants, belts studded with silver, metal bracelets around their wrists. The conventionality of style and fantasy with which people into this form of sex expressed their violations of conventionality has always been astonishing to me. A few women were dressed in classic pornography style, with tight little skirts and lacy black camisoles or bras. One had on just a bra and g-string with garters and stockings. Several wore dog collars around their necks attached to leather leashes wound around their mistresses' wrists. They stood by passively with pouty lips and expressionless eyes as their owners opened their shirts and fondled their breasts in public. Sometimes their breasts or buttocks were offered to other women to touch, and when this was done they evinced no reaction either. Linda was popular, and everybody offered her their slaves. As she stroked them she would talk about them in the third person, telling the person who had given her permission to touch them how attractive, how soft, how obedient their slaves were.

"If you'd like, I could ask permission for you to touch somebody too," Linda said.

"No thanks."

"Are you scared?"

"No. They're too ugly." What bothered me even more than their looks was their apparent social class—rather, their apparent lack of social class. They looked like they lived in East L.A., or some cheap place in the Valley.

We went into the back room where the action, if any, usually took place. The walls were black, and as it was lit by only a dim red lamp it took me a few seconds to see what was going on. There were several sets of stocks—the kind Puritans used to punish sinners, with holes to secure the head and hands—and some basket-like leather seats hung on chains from the ceiling. On a shelf in the rear was your standard assortment of paddles, whips, riding crops.

A woman was standing on a little platform, her bottom naked, her head and hands held in place by the stock. She was surrounded by several women who took turns swatting her with a whip. There was no urgency to this, minutes seeming to go by between each stroke. One woman always stood by the head of the woman being whipped, stroking her brow, pushing her hair off her forehead, wiping off the sweat, talking to her through the moans and telling her how beautiful and sweet and responsive she was.

We watched for a while, then the woman holding the whip offered it to me. I would have preferred to just watch but Linda had told me that if anyone asked me to do something I should do it; if I refused to participate I would make everyone uncomfortable, perhaps might even be asked to leave. Women were still a little touchy about this kind of sex, it had a very bad name—not just in the world but in the women's and even the lesbian movement. It was the big philosophical issue at the moment. Surely I must have read the articles.

"Actually, I don't buy that kind of magazine."

"You should. This kind of sex is really the last frontier. Dealing with this is just as difficult as coming out."

"I didn't know you were out," I had said to Linda.

Feeling curious, but not the least sexual, I took the whip. It had a nice, balanced feel. I raised my arm, then flicked it rather gently. You could barely hear the whip land on the woman's ass.

"You can do it harder," she said.

I tried again. Again, it was too gentle.

"Do it harder," the other women told me. "Don't be afraid of hurting her." *Harder*: the word sounded odd in their mouths.

After a few more strokes I began to get into it, and the woman I was hitting began to moan and say "ow." It was gratifying, though not immensely so. Soon an empathy— for the pain I was inflicting on her and the connection we were making through it—began to manifest itself in my body, so that I had my first flickerings of arousal. I no longer cared that she wasn't attractive, and the idea of running my hand over her face or caressing her breast no longer seemed so revolting.

After a while I was told to give the whip to someone else. I was about to leave the room when Linda grabbed my arm.

"Now you," she said.

"What?"

"You want to," she said. "I can tell."

"No."

"Ha!" She began to stroke my thighs. I'm not attracted to Linda, but I felt this searing flash go through me. Then her hand moved to my crotch. "I can feel the heat through your pants."

"Linda . . ." I pushed her hand away.

She grabbed my arms and pinned me against a wall near where we were standing. She was strong, but perhaps if I had really tried I could have pushed her away. But I shut my eyes and let her continue to caress me.

"You want me to, don't you?"

"No."

She laughed. "You sure fooled me."

"Not here."

"What's wrong with here?"

I leaned forward to whisper in her ear. "For one thing, the women are so ugly."

"They're not so bad," said Linda. "What about the one over there, you don't think she's attractive?"

"No."

"Or her?"

"No. I can honestly say there's not one person in this place I feel like having sex with," I said. Then I realized I might be insulting Linda. "I mean, not counting you. You're my friend." Then I realized Linda might be thinking I was making a pass at her, so I added. "Not that I'm attracted to you. God, you know what I mean, it's too complicated to explain."

"It's what you do that's important, not necessarily the people you do it with," said Linda. "You have very nice legs," she said, still stroking me. "Why don't you relax and see what happens?"

"I can't. Not in public."

"But you're wet, I can feel it," she said. "Will it be easier if I put a blindfold around your eyes so you don't have to see what's happening?" She touched my breast.

"Okay," I whispered.

"Wait a minute. I'll be right back."

I stood there, self-conscious, as if she were still propping me up, my eyes shut so I could not see the other women who might be looking at me.

"I don't want you to open your eyes, but move your head forward a bit," said Linda. I moved my head forward, and she slipped a blindfold over my head. "Is that better?" she asked.

"Yes."

"Now I want you to unzip your pants."

"I can't do that."

"You have to," she said.

I unzipped my pants. I felt foolish with them slightly open, and did not know whether I should push them down more or not. I didn't want to ask because that would look too eager. I almost wished my hands were tied so I would not have to worry about these things.

"Now I'm going to take you by the hand and lead you someplace where you'll be a little more comfortable."

"I'm scared my pants are going to fall down and I'll trip."

"Hold my hand and you'll be all right."

We walked a number of steps, then she told me to stop. She pushed my pants down so they were around my ankles. I couldn't remember what underpants I had worn that day and I was worried they had holes in them, or the crotch was pinkish-brown from blood I hadn't quite been able to wash out from my period. I told myself it was dark in the room and they wouldn't be able to see my underpants anyway. Then I began to worry that maybe she had brought me to the other room.

"We're still in the back room, aren't we?" I asked Linda.

"Relax," said Linda.

"I don't want to be up front. People might recognize me."

"This is a very safe environment," said Linda. "Whoever's here is only going to deal with you with love. Now I want you to lean over."

"But I'll fall!"

"No. There's something here. You'll be more comfortable."

I was draped over an object that felt like a pommel horse. It was covered with suede and had many smells in it. My mouth lay against it but I tried not to touch it with my lips so I would not catch the diseases that were surely nesting there. I was scared I was going to sneeze or have to blow my nose or even pee.

Linda began stroking my thighs. She began telling me how beautiful I was, how soft and compliant. I spread my legs a little so she could touch between them, though I did it in a way that I hoped would look like I was just shifting my weight. "Oh, that's nice," she said. She touched the bottom of my underpants. "You're incredibly wet," she said. "Do you know that? . . . I said, do you know that?" I nodded. "Now I want you to lift yourself up a little . . ." She raised me off the horse and pulled down my underpants. She ran her fingers up the backs of my thighs again, then began to lightly touch my ass. "What a pretty ass she has," she said. "Isn't this a pretty ass? See how it moves towards me when I touch it." And it did; I couldn't help myself, although whether it was because I was so turned on or because I was being hypnotized by her commands I was unable to tell. Now that Linda was talking about me in the third person the fact that I was in a club returned to the forefront of my attention and I realized there was a hum of voices around us and that they had been there for some time; I had just blocked them out. They were talking about me in the same calm tones they had used a little earlier in talking about the girl who had been in the stocks—how sweet and docile and vulnerable I looked lying there, how pretty my ass was and how it would look even prettier the next day when it was black-and-blue. "Go ahead, touch her, she doesn't mind," said Linda, and I felt the hands of strangers, the different hands of strangers, moving up my thighs and caressing my ass. Occasionally they would just brush by my crotch.

"She's really wet," they said.

"She's cherry," explained Linda.

"Oh, this is your first time," one said to me. I tried to

nod, but it was difficult in the position I was in. She put her hand on my neck and gently stroked it. "We know how you feel," she said. It was very soothing. "Don't worry. We won't do anything you don't want. You know that, don't you?" I tried to nod again, but she kept talking, and I realized she wasn't doing this so much to get an answer as to soothe me by the sound of her voice. I felt soothed. It was really very nice to be talked about like that, in such complimentary tones, in a way that I was not usually talked about unless I had done something extraordinarily witty or wonderful. But for once nothing seemed to be expected of me except to lie there.

I felt a sting across my ass. I assumed it was Linda's hand. I said "ow," more out of surprise than pain. My thighs were stroked again, and I trembled, waiting for the stroke. When it didn't come I was almost disappointed. I twitched my ass.

"See how she wants it," said someone.

"Oh yes. She's quite the little femme."

Again I felt the hand. It hurt more this time but I was expecting it and I didn't say anything. A finger tickled the hair in my ass, then slid down to my crotch.

"She's very wet."

"She'd probably beg for it if we stopped."

"You could tell she was that way when she walked in."

"People who act tough are always the biggest femmes."

"Ow!" I said. This time the hand really hurt. Then the spanks began to come more quickly. I realized my "ows" were due not so much to the intensity of the strokes as to their unpredictability. In a way I wanted to keep saying "ow," to let them know they were hurting me, but I didn't want to say it too much, in case they would stop. Then I thought about how crazy it was that even in here, when everything was being done for my pleasure, all I could think about was what kind of response I was supposed to make. Was there never a moment in my entire life when I could just relax?

I don't know whether it was the lecture or the hypnotic rhythm of the strokes, but after a while my mind stopped its chattering, and I was in a different kind of space, the one that exists while you're in a dream or watching a totally engrossing movie, and there's nothing to do but calmly witness the events going on all around you.

It was totally peaceful. I wanted to go to sleep. When they stopped I felt bereft, as if I had been chucked out of paradise.

"You can go on," I told Linda. "I'm okay."

"You've had enough."

She removed the blindfold, and I was forced to look at the women around me. They were still ugly, and though I felt more empathy for them than I had before, I wasn't sure whether this made it better or worse.

The next day I felt terribly depressed. I wanted to expunge my thoughts in water but the blue marks on my ass and thighs made me too embarrassed to go to the health club and swim. When Linda went to visit Judy I realized I was jealous—not of either of them but of the acts that went on between them. I knew on my own I would not have the courage to do such things. I lay in bed most of the day and slept, then I took the red-eye home.

I hadn't talked to Linda for almost a year when I received a creamy, engraved, stiff card inside a creamy, engraved, stiff envelope informing me that the former Ms. Linda Birnbaum of Westwood and Dr. Henry Goldberg of Beverly Hills were pleased to announce their marriage. The receipt of this note made it safe for me to contact

Linda again. In the course of the conversation I asked her if she had shared the details of her life as Duchess La Jeanne with her new husband.

"Oh no," she said. "I stopped that stuff when Jack and I broke up, soon after you were here. I realized it wasn't me at all." She told me that her son had stopped peeing all over the bathroom soon after Jack had moved out and that, as there was currently no extra room in Henry's house, her sculpture was temporarily on hold until they could build her a studio in his garage. One other thing. Henry had no children, and she was trying to get pregnant. At her age this was difficult, and she went into a long litany about bilirubens and luteal phase deficiencies and b.b.t. curves. It was both boring and reassuring, and served exactly the same conversational function as discussions of one's latest therapy session had in the old days.

When I hung up the phone I was both relieved and disappointed to discover I had been right, that deep down Linda was, as I had always thought, a nice Jewish girl. I realized also that, for some reason, no matter what I did or did not do, I was not, and this both relieved and disappointed me too.

caroline

The first time I saw Caroline she was sitting on a bar stool. I looked at her and smiled. She looked at me but did not smile. The calm coldness of her gaze seemed to create an island around her and me in which the noise and visual chaos of the bar disappeared. Words flashed through my mind, familiar ones about longing, and sadness, and love. When I went to talk to her, she responded in a half-bored way that made me think she wasn't interested in me. But I had nothing to lose by asking her to go home with me, and she surprised me by saying, oddly, yes.

I have been surprised in just this way before.

We climbed the steps to my apartment. I was still poor then, but she had ignored my suggestion about going to her place. She looked like she had more money than me, but perhaps I was mistaken. Or maybe she liked to slum. Why not? I did myself. More likely she was living with someone—a husband even. She didn't look gay. That was why I liked her.

Despite a certain awkwardness between us in bed, I was very excited. I think awkwardness excited me. In my self-consciousness I could never tell whether or not the other person was excited too. All night it was like this. I felt like I was a wet and disgusting human being. I felt my hands were like paws on her breast. I felt like telling her I loved her, and if she had told me she loved me I would not have been all that surprised. That is, the words might have surprised me, but not the thought.

On the other hand, it seemed as likely—or more so—that she would tell me that I was a terrible lover, boring, a creep, that she was having a bad time and never wanted to see me again.

"Would you like my number?" I asked her in the morning. After hours of wrong positions, just when I had fallen into some mildly unpleasant dream, I had heard her get up and start to get dressed. I didn't want her to leave, but my resentment at her waking me up and the tug of my dream kept me in bed too long to stop her.

"All right," she said, as if considering. I gave her my number and asked her for hers. There were more than the usual number of digits. "Work," she explained, in response to my look. "My extension." I was about to ask her what she did, as much to prolong her stay as because of any inherent interest in the question, when I remembered I had asked her this the night before. I remembered the question, but not the answer. It is often like this. But I doubted whether she would understand this if I told her.

I decided to wait several days before calling her. The sexual fever I was in was pleasant, and I was worried it might disappear if I saw her again. It did not occur to me she would call me, but she did. She invited me to dinner at an expensive restaurant.

This invitation didn't make me as happy as it should have. There are times I enjoy eating, but never when I'm supposed to, and the idea of having to pretend to enjoy this fancy meal depressed me. Then, I was disturbed that she had called me before I called her. It was not the usual sequence. First I wondered if there was something wrong with her, then I wondered if there was something wrong with me. By the time I was to meet her I was in a fairly bad mood. The idea that she would spend that much money to take me out to dinner was disconcerting. A woman who could afford to do that shouldn't even have been in the bar where I met her. These things, which in the abstract should have made me like her, made me distrust her.

I thought about calling her to change the time or the date, but I didn't; I felt in the thrall of a peculiar lassitude. I resented her for this too. All in all, I entered the restaurant feeling more like a martyr than someone invited to a meal in one of the city's most famous restaurants. Of course I didn't have the proper clothing, and the maître d' informed me with his eyes not just that he knew it, but that he knew I knew it too.

Caroline was seated with a group of people at a large round table. There was a space on her left but she motioned me to a seat across from her. She announced my name, and then the names of the people who were already seated at the table. They nodded their heads slightly at the mention of their names, then resumed their discussions. I wanted people to ask me what I did so I could tell them I was a writer, but like most New Yorkers they were more interested in who they knew than who they didn't. They were discussing the "rag" business, by which they meant not rags but clothing. Gradually the table filled, and the waiter came over to take our orders. I listened carefully to hear whether the others were ordering appetizers and salad. When it was my turn, Caroline offered suggestions as to what was particularly good on the menu. She didn't do this for anybody else, and it seemed to me she was doing it not so much out of friendliness as to point out to the others the fact that I had never before eaten in this restaurant. Some people joined in seconding her suggestions, and others disagreed violently. And yet I knew they didn't care. We seemed to have been brought together for a purpose everybody knew about but myself.

For a long time the table had been cleared, yet nobody came to ask us about coffee or dessert. I thought it strange that after such an expensive meal we were not to be allowed to order coffee or dessert. Then a group of waiters erupted from the kitchen, carrying a cake with a candle on it; they stopped at our table and began singing happy birthday to Caroline. Usually people seem embarrassed in such situations, but she acted calm and pleased, if slightly bored. The waiter asked her to make the first cut on the cake, then they took the plate back to their trolley and cut it up in pieces and put them on our plates. Nobody seemed interested in eating the cake except me.

While this had been happening one of the men had left the table; he now returned with a bunch of presents that had been hidden in the coatroom. Apparently everyone had brought Caroline a present except me. The presents were opened individually with much fuss and exclamation. Most of them seemed faddish, useless, and expensive. "I didn't know it was her birthday," I announced, rather softly, to the table at large. "Of course not," the person on my right replied.

After the coffee cups had been taken away Caroline went to the bathroom, and the waiter immediately brought the bill over to a short, rather feminine man who had been seated to her immediate right. He announced the total in a voice that covered much of the vocal register, then told everybody what to chip in. I felt ridiculous and angry; I had only twenty dollars in my pocket. "I can pay by credit card," I told him. "Oh no, that's not necessary," he said. I was grateful but also irritated by this; just because I was dressed in a more downtown style, did that necessarily mean I was so much poorer than everybody else?

With the paying of the check I assumed the party was over, but no one got up to leave; eventually, sambuco and more coffee were ordered. People continued to talk to me oddly, as if I were a recently discharged mental patient they had been told to be kind to. Finally everyone stood up to kiss Caroline goodbye. I tried to do this last, in case she wanted to spend the night with me. I did not especially feel like spending the night with her, but I felt obligated in some sense to try and reciprocate for this meal—even though, as it turned out, she was not paying for it. She seemed strange, distant, wholly unconnected with the woman I had slept with a few nights before. "I hope you had a good time," she said.

"It was a wonderful party," I told her. "Thank you for inviting me. I didn't know it was your birthday."

"I thought you might be interested in meeting some of my friends."

"Yes. They seemed very nice," I lied. As usual, I felt awkward around her. "Are you tired? Or do you want to go somewhere?"

"You mean, like your apartment?"

I nodded.

"No, I don't think that would be right."

Of course I could not tell her I hadn't really wanted to spend the night with her either. But as I walked out of the restaurant I remembered the clumsy excitement I had experienced when I was with her, and I realized I was just hiding my desires from myself, so that I would not fall down on my knees in front of her and bark like a dog. I leaned against a car to wait for her.

"You're still here," she announced when she came out of the restaurant a few minutes later. Several friends, including the man with the high vocal register, were still with her.

"Yes," I said.

"We're going to Barclay's, if you'd like to come. Is that all right with you?" she asked the little man.

"It's your night, darling," he said. Or was it, "your life"?

There was some inexplicable but apparently humorous problem about the limousine, so we all piled into a taxi. Barclay lived in an expensive building by the UN that overlooked the river. It was all steel and glass, and I hated it almost as much as I hated his apartment: the soft Italian leather couches, the paintings (some of which I recognized) on the walls, white circles of light the size of quarters illuminating appropriate areas of sculpture and flowers, the mound of white powder on a glass plate. I hated the gleaming kitchen with its food processor that rose out of the counter when you pressed a button, the giant bathroom with its steam room and jacuzzi, the mini-gym that occupied half his bedroom, but most of all I hated myself, for allowing my emotions to be disturbed by trivial things such as this.

"Beautiful view, isn't it?" Caroline asked me. She had joined me on the terrace as I stood looking downtown and across the East River. Lights were everywhere: from the buildings of New York, the cars on the avenues and the Drive, the stars overhead, and all of these reflected in the whitecaps in the river. In its black-and-whiteness, it was a little bit like an inexpensive downtown art movie, and a little bit like a screwball comedy from the thirties.

"Not bad," I said, though I hated the glittery coercion of it.

"Of course it's a bit much. But that's Barclay for you."

"People like that are always like that."

"No, they're not." She looked into my eyes and then kissed me. It was a terrible kiss, but I felt my pants get wet. "I bet you'd like to take me home and beat the shit out of me."

"Maybe."

She went back inside. When I followed her in she was talking to Barclay. She proceeded to ignore me for the next half hour.

If she hadn't said what she had I would have left. But she had.

■ ■ ■

"What are you doing?" she asked, when I walked over to my couch with a leather belt swinging from my right hand an hour and a half later.

"I don't own any paddles or whips."

"If you don't drop that this second I'm going to split."

I put the belt down. The idea of having to beat her had somewhat depressed me, but now the idea of not beating her depressed me too. "I thought you wanted me to."

"Are you crazy?" she asked. "It must be the coke. People like you aren't used to good coke."

"My friends have good coke," I said in a defensive whine.

In the moonlight coming through my windows I stared at her profile. There was something unearthly about it, white and statue-like, over-planned. She wore stockings under her skirt. All this reminded me of something distant, both pleasureful and disturbing. Perhaps it was the days I thought of myself as a woman.

I fought off the impulse to tell her she was beautiful. I felt she would like me better if I treated her badly. But instead of being forceful and rough, I let my fingers creep tentatively around her neck, as if we were high school kids on a first date. Again our lips touched awkwardly. I decided this time I wouldn't invite her into the bedroom unless she did certain things to me, the kind of things she would normally do for people more assertive than me.

"You know, you're the first woman I've ever been with," she said.

"I know."

"I'm not sure whether I like it."

"Of course you do."

"I'm not sure whether I like it with men either."

Psychopathology does not appeal to me, and I was getting uncomfortable. I liked normal women who looked like women who slept with lots of men.

"Cut it out," I said. I took her in my arms. Her body felt incredibly cold, like a corpse. I couldn't decide whether I loved her or hated her or whether she bored me in a way I tended to confuse with interest. The decision seemed crucial, yet I knew also it didn't matter, that all I really cared about was that I find something new to distract me from myself. What mattered? I couldn't remember. These were terrible thoughts, and I reached out and touched her lips with my tongue, not as in a kiss, but simply as a kind of touching. I ran my tongue up and down the ridges of her lips, then I moved it inside her mouth, along the gums on top of her mouth and then the bottom, and then inside and finally on the roof of her mouth, though it was difficult to reach this with my slightly-less-than-normal-sized tongue, and I thought how strange and interesting the human body is, that there were all these places and cavities for one's tongue or finger or toes to explore, and how we usually neglected most of them. I refused to do the obvious, and instead gave her an orgasm by licking first the inside, then the outside of her knee.

Before she left I asked her for her home phone number. After a slight hesitation, she gave it to me. She told me to hang up if anyone else answered, but no one ever did.

Although there were things about the relationship that bothered me, I called her every day the next few weeks. For some reason I felt it was my duty to continue asking her out until she decided to stop seeing me. Although we occasionally had dinner with her friends, I never got to

know them any better than that first night. They all had
the same expensive and impersonal objects in their houses,
as if they took the chic and glossy magazines they sub-
scribed to seriously. I had always thought one of the
advantages of being rich was that one did not have to take
these magazines seriously. They seemed to have no interest
in reading my books. I think I was more pleased than
angered that they did not read them, as this gave me an
acceptable reason to dislike them. I asked a number of
times, but she never let me spend the night in her apartment.

Although theoretically Caroline and I grew to know
each other better, it still felt awkward each time when I
first touched her, as if in the interim I had somehow
forgotten who she was. But the fact of the awkwardness
was becoming familiar, which began to change it into
something else. Less and less did I get a glimpse of what
it reminded me of, something that was just on the tip of
my memory, which to remember was the real reason I
think I was with her. It seemed the things I had been
doing had never been done before, at least in combination
with the thoughts I was having as I was doing them—
which is perhaps all that newness is in the human plane.
And yet the newness was archetypal, familiar, a bit boring,
as if I knew not the content but the form. I wanted to
protect her from the world, and yet I knew that in the
important ways she was far stronger than me. Though I
very much wanted to, I could not bring myself to tell her
what I was thinking. What if she were more similar to me
than I thought? What if I frightened her as much as she
frightened me?

It was all about her profile—not the one I saw now, but

the one I had seen sitting on the barstool the night I met her.

I felt that if I could understand the essence of her looks and her coldness, I would know everything I would need to know to become the human being I had always wanted to become. I realized her coldness did not upset me. I welcomed it. It gave space to my own to disappear and die.

One night while we were lying in my bed she told me her husband was coming back, that she wouldn't be able to see me any more.

"Oh," I said. I had suspected but hadn't been sure she had a husband. I moved away from her so she wouldn't see the tears forming in my eyes. I was hoping she would touch me on the shoulder and roll me towards her, so she would see them.

"He's been on a business trip," she explained.

"Kind of a long one, isn't it?" As I turned towards her, I tried to force the tears out of my eyes and down my face. This is difficult to do and I could only squeeze out a few drops. I felt it would be cheating to rub them away with my fingers in order to call her attention to them.

"You didn't really think there was a future between us, did you?"

"No." It was true, but I tried to make it sound like a lie. "I'm sorry I never got to see the inside of your apartment."

"It's really quite nice," she said.

Several months later I ran into Barclay at some benefit a friend had given me last-minute tickets to. "What are you doing here?" he trilled bitchily. "I thought you didn't have any money."

"Empty seats look bad," I explained. "Probably half the people got in free." I was exaggerating to make him feel rotten for wasting his money. Only later did I realize that the only people who spent money on benefits were people to whom it meant nothing. Despite the evenings we had spent together, all we had in common was Caroline. I was determined I wouldn't ask him how she was, but he kept standing there.

"How's Caroline?" I finally gave in. "Is she getting on with her husband?"

"Her *husband*?" he laughed. "God, isn't she too much?"

It was impossible to tell who was the liar: Barclay, Caroline, perhaps even myself. I had always felt the truth resided in my body and not my words. Maybe I had invented some or all of what Caroline had said, as I had invented a story for myself about the awkwardness between her body and mine that I had used to convert this awkwardness into something exciting and powerful—at least for a while. At least for awhile this invention had been so strong that in some way I had convinced her to make it hers. I called it "love," but of course that was an invention too.

morocco

It was our last night in Fez. Although the guide had assured us time and again that no nightclubs were open in this holy city during Ramadan, nonetheless he managed to find us a place where Alice could witness fire-dancing. This was a very special thing, he assured us: the club open only for the benefit of the beautiful Americans; if caught, the proprietors could go to jail for many years. Or was this only if they were caught drinking? As with everything in Morocco, we assumed the explanation was a justification for the absurdly high cover charge. Nevertheless, we were glad to go. In fact, the club was almost empty, with only a few foreigners and local girls sitting together at one table—oddly, all of them wearing Western clothing. A male Moroccan danced holding a torch. Touristy or not, it was good, yet after a few moments my eyes soon began to close. I grow sleepy early when I travel, overcome by the stimulation of new places. "Do you want to dance?" the guide asked me when the man was done.

"No thank you. Maybe later," I said politely. Alice and Susan, of course, did not dare dance together in such a place.

"Perhaps you would like to now?" the guide asked a few minutes later.

"I'm a little tired. Thank you just the same."

"You think I'm not a good dancer? I'm a very good dancer. Would you like to see?" He held out his hand.

"I'm sure you are."

"You don't like me?" he asked, with a sad face.

"Yes, very much," I assured him.

"Then why won't you dance with me?" After several minutes of this, I confessed I wasn't interested in men.

"Not interested in men? What do you mean? Do you mean you are a virgin?" he asked in astonishment. Naturally, we were speaking in French.

"*Je préfère les femmes*," I told him.

"*Préfère les femmes? Qu'est-ce que c'est? Je n'ai jamais de ma vie entendu une telle chose!*"

We continued in this vein for a while, with me asserting my miraculous preference, and him professing to be astonished by it. After realizing I would not abandon my predilections and spend the night with him, abruptly he changed his tune. "Okay, I'll speak to the owner's sister for you," he said. "Perhaps she will spend the night with you."

"Which one is she?" I asked. He pointed to the table where the other occupants in the bar were sitting, but I couldn't tell which woman he meant. One seemed quite beautiful, so I nodded. It had been so long, no doubt I would have nodded in any case.

The guide joined them at their table. He turned back to look at me, pointed; they looked at me and smiled. In a few minutes the guide came over and said that the bar owner's sister had invited me to join them at their table.

"Will she go home with me?"

"I don't know. It's up to you. Probably not. It's Ramadan."

Despite this, I saw no harm in joining them. They asked my name, my nationality, and the names of the friends I was traveling with. To my disappointment, the bar owner's sister was not the beautiful one. However, the idea of going home with a Moroccan woman, of whatever appearance, had begun to excite me: partly because I had never been with a Moroccan, and partly on account of the difficulty—which was, of course, increased by its being Ramadan. I tried to make more general conversation, but in my fatigue my French, as usual, began to disappear. Even when they managed to decipher my questions, I had to ask them to repeat their answers several times. Soon I began to smile and nod my head automatically at everything they said. Naturally I could not blame them for reverting to Arabic. In their own language they became more animated; nearly every word evoked much laughter. I smiled along with them, though almost surely they were laughing at my expense. I was the only one drinking, and my paranoia grew.

"My friend wants to know, do you want to go home with her?" the beautiful one suddenly asked.

"What?" I was sure I had misunderstood, but the guide repeated the offer. His French was the easiest for me to understand.

"Tell her I'd rather go home with *her*," I told him.

They spoke a bit, then the guide told me: "They live together." Was he suggesting the possibility of a threesome, or was I being too subtle? I began to sweat.

I told Susan and Alice I was leaving with the Moroccan women. "Do you think it's safe?" they asked. I shrugged my shoulders; they knew the name of the nightclub and the guide. "The younger one's pretty," said Alice.

"Pretty! She's beautiful!"

"Have a good time." I assured them I would. In any case, I promised to be at the hotel no later than noon the next day for our drive to Meknes. After thanking the guide, and receiving more smirks from the bar owner and the woman he was with, I followed the women out of the bar.

The square was empty and dark. Only now did it occur to me to feel scared. After all, I had no idea where the women lived. Perhaps it was like the home I had been to in the old quarter in Tangier, several floors around an open courtyard protected from the rain by clear plastic, the bathroom merely a hole in the ground with an indescribable smell. "Do you live in the medina?" I asked.

"Oh no," they laughed. I felt reassured, though our footsteps clicked loudly against the stone.

"Is it far?"

"No."

I tried to put my friends' fears—and my own—out of my mind. After all, we were nowhere near the old quarter; surely I was too old to be sold into white slavery. We stopped in front of a modern building several stories high, the kind you might find anywhere. We walked up an external staircase to the second floor; at the end of the corridor were two doors. The one who had invited me took out her key, and I followed her and her girlfriend into their apartment.

The floor was parquet, the furniture Swedish modern; even with the ubiquitous Moroccan pillows, I could have been in any sparsely decorated European apartment. A little girl, perhaps seven years old, was sleeping on the couch. The beautiful one woke her up and carried her into one of the two rooms that opened onto the other end of the living room. Almost immediately, she returned with a pipe.

"Do you like hashish?" she asked.

"Very much." They offered me some, and I began to get high, though I sensed they were smoking along with me just to be polite. Then they brought out a bottle of wine. In my nervousness I was glad to accept it, although I would not have had I known that, even now, in the privacy of their apartment, where they surely would not have been arrested, they would still refuse to drink with me.

We tried to make conversation. The ugly one spoke to the beautiful one in Arabic, who then spoke to me in French, after which she would translate back into Arabic for the other. With the wine and hashish on top of my fatigue, this was even worse than in the bar. We tried switching to English, but their English was worse than my French. Finally we ended up leaning back against the cushions and smiling at each other.

When it was around two-thirty, the ugly one got up to prepare dinner. Now that the necessity for the clumsy double translation was gone, I tried to satisfy my curiosity concerning the relationship between the women. But the beautiful one professed not to or did not in fact understand me, and instead brought out photographs of herself, her friend, and the little girl—who as it turned out was her daughter. I complimented her first on her daughter and then on the apartment, whose cleanliness and modernity astonished me. In retrospect such an attitude seems absurd, for I had seen many modern buildings in Tangier, but of course while sightseeing one usually focuses on the decrepit and old.

Dinner was chicken with olives and other vegetables over rice, served out of a brown clay pot. My place was easy to spot—the one with the silverware. When I tried to eat with my hands they laughed at the mess I made. A friendly laugh, almost surely, but again I began to feel paranoid. Though the meal was delicious I had to force myself to swallow, partly because, unlike the Moroccans, who couldn't so much as have a drink of water until sunset, I had already eaten my three meals, and partly because I recalled a Paul Bowles story about the predilection Moroccans had for poisoning each other. I told myself that the three of us were eating out of the same pot, and, in any case, however disappointed at my lack of conversation or inability to eat properly with my fingers they might be, this was surely insufficient reason to murder me. I finally managed to clear my plate, though I refused a second helping. The women ate quickly and efficiently, scooping up food and gravy with pieces of bread.

Both because I wanted to appear polite, and also because I wanted to see the kitchen, I got up to help clear the table. It would have been odd had the kitchen not been as modern as the rest of the apartment; nonetheless, for some reason this astonished me. I simply could not believe they owned a refrigerator as good as any I have ever owned. Even more amazing was what was inside: several six-packs of beer and a carton of milk on the otherwise empty shelves. Above the refrigerator was the liquor cabinet. They offered me scotch, gin, Cointreau. A drink would have helped with my paranoia (or at least dulled the sensation of it), but they weren't having any, so I shook my head and said I'd prefer to drink mint tea with them.

"You like mint tea?"

"Very much, yes. I would make it in America, only there mint is very expensive."

"How expensive?"

"A dollar for a small bunch." I bunched my hands to show them the amount.

"No!"

"Yes!" I saw them disbelievingly calculate the sum they would need to drink mint tea every day in America—for all I knew, this could be the equivalent of the average Moroccan's daily income. "When we drink mint tea in America, we drink it out of tea bags." They did not seem to understand this word, so I explained. "A tea bag, you know, it's a little package, like Sanka comes in." They looked doubtful, and I couldn't blame them; how could they not, they who shoved huge fistfuls of fresh green mint into glasses, then poured hot water over it?

"Things are very expensive in America, aren't they?"

"Yes." I told them what my rent was, and the price of a meal in a good restaurant, and what it cost to see a movie.

"When you sleep with a woman in America, how much do you have to pay her?"

I had been wondering how I was going to broach the object of our encounter, so I was glad the subject had come up, in however oblique a context. I explained that, in America, when I slept with a woman, I did not have to pay her. That is, I did not have to pay her unless she were the kind of woman you had to pay—though I did not tell them this.

"Impossible!" They thought I was kidding. "It is very expensive, no?"

"No," I assured them, "in America, women sleep with each other for free."

"Surely not!" they protested.

"Oh yes!"

"But it is a bad thing?"

"Some people think so. But there are bars where we can meet each other. And then, sometimes, one sleeps with a friend." I smiled at them, as if to indicate a kinship with their relationship.

At the word "bar" they perked up. "This bar, is very expensive, no?"

"No. Less than the nightclub. Perhaps a few dollars. Sometimes it is free and you only have to pay for the drinks."

"These are very expensive?"

"No. The same as at other bars, more or less."

"More or less?" the beautiful one asked in confusion.

"That means 'the same.' But often, you know, I meet women at parties. That is how I met the last woman I lived with."

Much talking between them in Arabic. Clearly they were puzzled. By now it was quarter to four. I had been up since nine the previous morning, and I yawned.

"Would you like to go to bed?" the beautiful one asked. They led me to a room. In it was a double bed and a table with a telephone on it. They gave me a clean, folded towel. I prepared to wait, but they indicated I should use the bathroom ahead of them. The little girl was already in bed in the other bedroom. I washed slowly, giving the ugly woman—and perhaps the beautiful one as well—time to undress and be naked in my bed by the time I returned to my room.

But they were still in the other bedroom, talking to the

little girl. I called out *"Bon soir"* and entered my room. Under the covers, naked, with the light off but the door open, I waited for them.

After a while the sounds of dripping water and toilet flushing stopped, and then the lights—from the bathroom, the hall, finally their bedroom—clicked off. In the thrill of not knowing precisely who would appear, or when, I grew wet. My excitement was so intense it was almost painful, and I had to breathe slowly and deeply to calm myself. Then I heard them talking softly through the wall.

I assumed they were quieting the little girl, somehow explaining to her the presence of this odd guest. Eventually all was silent. I waited patiently; no doubt they were making certain the little girl was asleep before joining me. But soon I began to grow restless. Both to occupy myself and to signal them I was still awake, I got up and turned on the light.

I looked around the room for a paper and pen. It had occurred to me to conceal a note in my clothing, in case something terrible happened to me during the night. But the table in the room had no drawers, and there was no night table or bureau. Even the closet was empty except for a few dresses on hangers. Nothing else—not even a store receipt or torn-off envelope—was in the room. Neither in the homes I had been to in the medina, nor here, had I ever seen anything remotely resembling an American-style desk. Didn't Moroccans have electric and phone bills to be paid, letters to write and bank statements to be saved?

In desperation I searched for something to read. Anything—a magazine or even a brochure—would have done. Finally, on a shelf near the bed, I found *The Story of O.* That is, *L'Histoire d'O,* for of course it was in French. But it was still a book, the kind of object that had succored me so often in the past, so I lay back on the bed and turned to the first page. It had been almost twenty years since I first read the novel, but a few of its images—and the memory of the effect it had had on me when I first read it in high school—were still vivid in my mind. It had been my first indication that the erotics of submission had occurred to minds other than my own—a fact that was, at the time, perhaps as disturbing as it was reassuring.

Although it is easier to read a foreign language than to speak or understand it, in my fatigue I found it almost impossible to decipher the French. The vocabulary was sophisticated, much more so than I would have suspected. As I struggled to keep my eyelids open, I wondered what was taking the Moroccans so long. Surely I had been alone for almost half an hour. Then the odd fact of this book being in the room—this book, of all possible books in the world—struck me. Knowing they would be delayed, had the women left the book here so I would get aroused as I waited for them? Acquiescent as always, I felt obliged to tackle the foreign words again. For a while I thought I was succeeding, then I realized I was not so much reading the words as remembering images from the movie, and making up other images—ones involving the women on the other side of the wall from where I lay. As time passed, I began to think: What if the presence of the book was in itself a kind of psychic sadism, whose sole aim was to frustrate me and keep me awake all night? Such a scenario seemed both insufficiently motivated and impossibly subtle—and yet, could the presence of the book in my room be merely a coincidence?

I put my ear to the wall. I thought I heard whispering, but perhaps it was just the sound of myself breathing. I decided I could wait no longer. I shut off the light, got out of bed, and knocked on the door of the neighboring room.

"*Qu'est-ce que c'est?*" I heard a sleepy voice demand.

"*Est-ce que vous allez faire l'amour avec moi?*" I said, in the words I had carefully debated. (*Vous* for the possibility of the plural threesome; though I regretted the loss of the intimate *tu*.)

"*Nous sommes endormies,*" I heard, or something like. So I returned to my bed. Whereupon in my frustration I bit off half a Valium, and tried to sleep.

The beautiful one woke me with a knock on the door. It was almost ten, and she had to take the little girl somewhere. I was relieved to have the morning's potential awkwardness alleviated by the necessity of haste; quickly I washed and dressed. The beautiful one told me the other woman had already left for work at the hospital, where she was a nurse. I was to meet her there for lunch, at noon. (That is, I assumed: *I* was to have the lunch, while she sat there hungrily eyeing me.)

"That's impossible. I have to go to Meknes with my friends."

"You can stay," she said.

"No," I said. "We've already made our reservations."

"I will tell her," she said doubtfully. "But she will be most sorry."

She opened the door. On the threshold I stopped. If I did not ask the question now, I never could. "You did not join me in my room last night," I said. "If you did not want to have sex with me" (*faire l'amour* I had to say), "why did you invite me home with you?"

"You are a stranger, you needed a place to sleep."

"That is very nice, and your apartment is nicer than the hotel. But my clothing was in my hotel. In America, when people invite people home with them, it is for the purpose of making love to them."

"I did not invite you. My friend invited you, so you must ask her her reason. Perhaps she will tell you over lunch."

I reiterated the impossibility of this, but I asked for the phone number at the hospital. "It is not good to call her there," she said. "You will never reach her." Only when I convinced her that in any case I would not meet her friend in person did she reluctantly give me the number. Why I insisted I don't know, for of course I never used it. As bad as my French was in person, over the phone it was worse. Even if I had managed to reach her, how could we have managed to talk to each other? For that matter, face to face, as she watched me eat, in what language could we have spoken? Without difficulty I found my hotel. Alice and Susan were still in bed. They professed great relief at my appearance, and told me how they had already planned their visit to the police, the gloomy phone call to my parents. As they had evidently until quite recently been happily engaged in other activities, I found these statements unconvincing.

"So what happened?" asked Susan.

"None of your business," I smiled mischievously.

Alice, always suspicious, was cleverer. "I knew it," she cried. "I bet Susan a dollar nothing happened!"

"I said, *it's none of your business.*" But of course, over breakfast (which we had to pester an understandably irritable—and hungry, and thirsty—café owner to make for us), I confessed my failure. "It was the beer in the fridge that gave them away," I said. "They might have had liquor around for the rest of the year" (unlike the stricter Moslem countries, Morocco in those days still permitted the consumption of alcohol—at least during times other than Ramadan), "but only whores would bother to keep the beer cold. For their customers."

"Why didn't you offer to pay them?" said Alice. "It couldn't have been all that much."

"I don't know," I said. I didn't, though I suppose it must be ascribed to my vanity, to the Moroccans' utter disbelief that in America you—meaning "I"—could get it for free.

We packed up and drove on to Meknes, where, for the first time in a week, we bought the *International Trib*. In a café, as twilight fell, we read how Thurmon Munson, the Yankee catcher, had crashed practicing touch-and-go's in his private jet. A private jet, baseball, Cleveland: worlds away from the men surrounding us in their movie-costume red fezzes and white dresses, irritable without their cigarettes and mint tea, waiting for the siren to signal the mad dash to the drinking fountains. It was Africa. Around midnight the women would appear, arm in arm, in their white hooded gowns, to catch the cool of the evening before preparing the pre-dawn meal. No matter how much I paid them, I would never find out what they did, in the privacy of their homes, by themselves.

fame

I had drunk too much the night before, and I was very tired. The makings of a beautiful sunset were there, but I was too lazy to get out of bed and walk the fifteen feet to the chair next to the window with the west view, so instead I lay in bed thinking about it until the sky was dark enough that I became conscious of the lights in the building across the street, and then I fell asleep. When I woke up at ten-thirty I was ravenous, and quickly made myself a peanut butter and jelly sandwich. I ate with my eyes half closed, as if I were still asleep. I liked the feeling, but nonetheless I drank a Coke to wake me up. It was a beautiful night, the air warm and moist the way I liked it, fabulous things hung in the air it would be crazy not to take advantage of. And yet, even as my body began to arouse itself, I felt a kind of nostalgia for the deep and pleasant fatigue I was yanking myself out of, for the illusion of potential pleasures that were surely more exciting than whatever real pleasures I might find. Depression began to overtake me, so that I half-wished the night were cold, rainy, unpleasant. Why should I be alone on such a beautiful evening? Why should I be forced to bear the heat arising from the pavements, when destiny surely intended for me to be at the beach, sitting by tropical palms, surrounded by cool and wealthy women in white dresses? How come I didn't even own a car, so that I could drive to Brooklyn and look at the buildings of Manhattan with a mixture of envy and contempt? No, I was stuck in the hot and dirty city, with people as pathetic and hopeless as me. I splashed some water on my face, grabbed my keys, stuffed a few dollars and my bank card into the back pocket of my jeans, and rolled my bike out to the elevator. My face was gritty from the dirt of the city settling on my sweat, but I didn't care—if I had to settle for whoever came my way, so did they. She.

The streets were crowded, as they always are on hot nights in New York. Around Canal cars were approaching gridlock; one guy got out of a taxi, left the door open, and started walking uptown. "Hey you—" the cab driver shouted, and ran out to follow him. When I rode past I saw the meter was still on. But the cars started moving, and the cars in back of the taxi started cursing the driver, so he got back in the car. Even the pedestrians were crazy. As they tottered drunk out of restaurants, laughing and waving at me, I had to repress an urge to knock them over.

I locked the bike and went into the Boxcar. The women looked better than usual, but an unendurable impatience nonetheless came over me. Perhaps it was merely the heat, elevating my body temperature to a warmth that I mistook for something else. But I wanted someone different, the kind of person who would never walk into this bar.

I wandered outside to the street. A few tables were set up on the pavement. I plopped myself down in the only empty chair and began peeling the metallic paper off the top of my beer bottle. It was partially a nervous habit, but I couldn't stand the taste of metal in my mouth. No one else ever seemed to do this; I guess it didn't bother them. I don't know why not; sometimes it seemed I was different from everybody else in the world. I listened to the women at my table talking about a house some friends of theirs were renting in Cherry Grove. They all knew each other, they were happy and young and I hated them—partly because they were young and happy, partly because of the house in Cherry Grove, but mostly because, although I was right at their table, I was invisible to them.

Knowing it was fruitless, I unlocked my bike and headed over to La Donna. Since you had to pay five dollars to get in, I tended to think of the women there as ritzier than those at the Boxcar. But what was five dollars? and on hot nights like this, when you didn't have to bother about coatchecks and rain, the populations of the bars exchanged themselves like animals searching for better forage. Still, I was restless, and the recollection of happy nights in this bar, back in the days when it was called the Mermaid, could still arouse the memory of nostalgia, if not nostalgia itself. The streets were even crazier than before, so that I regretted not having worn my helmet. But I couldn't bear the way people looked at you when you admitted it was a bicycle rather than a motorcycle helmet you were carrying.

I walked to the back of the bar (that is, the space that was the room) to see if I knew anybody at the dance floor or tables, then I headed back to the bar (that is, the piece of varnished wood that is the physical bar) to buy a beer. Usually I stand by the jukebox, but someone with longish blond hair, slightly curling at the ends, had her legs wrapped around a barstool, a colorless bubbly drink in a tall glass with lime in it in front of her. Either it was something-and-tonic, or she was an alkie on the wagon. I walked back and sat down a seat away from her. She looked familiar as she idly swished the lime around in her glass, and I tried to place where I had met her. Rather, not met her, for this I would have remembered, but where I had seen her. It was not just that she was beautiful, but she was beautiful in a way that was just my type—classical features overlaid with the slightest hint of something trashy. Maybe it was just the faded, tight jeans and the man-styled oxford shirt—white from a distance but up close you could see stripes made by tiny dark-blue dots. Without makeup she looked so plain that at first I was not sure it was her. But when she saw me staring at her she smiled, and I saw the famous teeth, and there could be no doubt. It was the movie star—the one we all have a crush on—sitting alone one seat away from me at the bar of La Donna.

I moved over next to her. If the gods reject us there is no insult, so the shyness I experience around those whose attractions are equivocal did not come into play here. "Do you come here often?" I asked.

The famous smile. "No. Do you?"

"I heard you sometimes came here, but I never believed it." Again she played with her stirrer. "Are you with someone or—"

She shook her head. "Uh-uh."

What I really wanted to know was how come nobody

else was talking to her, but I felt asking this would be impolite. "Gin and tonic?" I asked.

She shook her head. "Vodka." I signaled Judy, the bartender, to come over. "You want another?"

"Do I look like I need one?" she laughed. She picked up her drink and almost finished it. So I ordered two. She put down a twenty and told Judy to keep the change.

"Let me," I said. Then I thought: how stupid, of course she can afford it more easily than me.

"Thanks sweetheart," Judy said, then winked.

I quickly drank my drink to give me courage, then said, "I know you must have heard this a thousand times before, but I think you're the most beautiful person in the world. If I could go to bed with anybody in the world it would be you." She didn't say anything. "I guess that's not a very original line . . ."

"It doesn't matter," she said, "I've heard them all."

"I used to fantasize what I would do if I ever saw you here—"

"Yeah?"

"First I'd buy you a drink"—I motioned to the drink—"and then another, and you'd get a little high, and after a while I'd ask you to dance. At first you'd refuse, because what if someone recognized you, but after the third or fourth drink you'd say 'what the hell?' and you'd let me take you by the hand and lead you to the dance floor.

"In the beginning the music would be fast so there wouldn't be that awkwardness, but every time the song ended I'd be worried a slow song would come on and you'd walk away, but I'd also be wanting a slow song to come on so I could pull you close to me. And then, finally, a slow song *would* come on and instead of leaving the dance floor you'd let me put my arms around you, and a little later you'd put your arms around me, and at that moment I'd be happier than I've ever been in my life."

I paused. She said nothing. I thought what I had said was very beautiful, and that perhaps she was digesting this.

"How sweet," she said. "But of course, you know, I'm just like everybody else."

"No you're not."

"Yes I am."

"Not to me," I said. "I watch that stupid movie"—and I named the picture, the one that had made her famous—"over and over again."

She laughed. "That was a long time ago."

"But you're more beautiful than ever."

"Do you really think so?"

"Of course. That's why nobody was talking to you just now. They're intimidated by you."

"But not you?"

"Oh no. I'm famous myself."

"Really? What's your name?" I told her. "That's odd. I've never heard of you."

"Well, maybe not so famous."

Again she laughed. Perhaps more than anything, I was impressed with her teeth. Nothing could be more starched, more perfect, more clean. They looked like she hadn't had a cavity in her life. I told myself that occasionally food had to get stuck between them, just like mine; still, I couldn't picture this. She could have been a toothpaste ad. She was drinking vodka, but when I thought of her mouth against mine, I imagined Crest.

I couldn't tell at all whether or not she was attracted to me. Oddly, the main quality that emanated from her was *niceness*. "Do you have a lover?" I asked.

"Kind of. But not really."

She seemed a little sad as she said this. I wanted to tell her I'd be happy to sleep at her feet for the rest of her life if that was what she wanted. But of course I couldn't. We fell silent again. I was trying to figure out what I should do next. Most people I knew wouldn't dance at La Donna; the dance floor was too small. But even a big dance floor would be no big deal to a movie star. Could anything be a big deal to a movie star? If so, I certainly couldn't supply it. But then, if she were looking for that, she wouldn't be here. "The music is terrible, but—" I tilted my head towards the dance floor.

"What the hell?" She stood up.

I'd been so entranced talking to her that for once I hadn't even looked to see if anyone was staring at us. As we walked to the dance floor I could feel my face grow red. But nobody seemed to notice her. Or perhaps, they were just pretending not to notice her. But in fact, I felt, they *didn't* notice her. This seemed incomprehensible, but wasn't life incomprehensible? Did I not complain about this very state of affairs all the time?

The music was fast. I have always felt it in some sense unfair to attempt to seduce people by dancing sexily, so I scarcely looked at her at all. My fear that she would stop dancing after the first dance didn't materialize, and eventually I began to feel more comfortable. I tried to get in that head where the relation of one's movements to the music is more important than impressing the other person, and I partially succeeded. Then the music slowed, and I remembered how in my fantasy she had let me pull her close, and I pulled her close. She did not resist.

She was taller than me, and I felt a little awkward with my arms around her starched shirt. What someone my size needs is to be held rather than to hold. I tried to bathe myself in her smells—mostly Clorox and a clean-smelling soap. Mentally I was happy, but I was too nervous to feel it in my body.

Then the music got terrible, the way it does when the DJ decides it's time for everybody to buy another drink, and we had to leave the dance floor.

"Can I get you something?" I asked, when we had seated ourselves again.

"Two vodka-and-tonics," she told Judy. Again she insisted on paying.

Our hands were on the bar. She had long strong fingers; in fact, a feeling of muscularity was present all the way up her thin arms. Her veins were more prominent than mine. We were about the same age, but next to her my hands— shorter, rounder, almost devoid of lines—seemed like a child's.

"You have beautiful hands," I said, then blushed. To listen to me you would not realize I was an interesting person. Unable to think of any topics with more general appeal, I began to tell her about myself: how I was a writer, how I loved to come to the bar to pick people up but that I rarely succeeded, how nonetheless I seemed to enjoy all this. She seemed mildly amused and sympathetic, whereas usually the people I revealed myself to in this fashion looked at me as if I were a jerk. No doubt it was stupid to reveal myself to them, but that was my particular kick: I wanted people to know my jerkiness and love me anyway. She asked me the names of the books I had written, and when she confessed she had not heard of them, I promised to send them to her.

"We could go get them now," she said.

"Now?" I echoed in astonishment.

"Unless you're busy." I saw the famous lips pulled back over the famous teeth in what was almost a smirk.

■ ■ ■

I was too embarrassed to mention I had ridden a bicycle to the bar, so I left it locked outside, hoping it would still be there in the morning. You may not be able to cut through a Kryptonite lock, but then you don't have to, you can knock off the bar at the end with a hammer in thirty seconds. In a way I almost hoped it would be stolen, so this could be part of my story, my sacrifice to the golden goddess whom I had managed to seduce with my looks and honeyed words. Horns were blaring in the sweaty streets, and it was hard to get a taxi. "Hi,——," the driver said conversationally to the movie star when we got in the cab, as if they were old buddies.

She leaned forward to look at his license. "Hi, Mike," she said in return. "You been driving long?"

"Long enough to know to go back to school." He was forty-one, studying the classics so he could teach Latin to high school students.

"I didn't know people studied Latin anymore."

"It's hopeless, but you got to put your finger in the dike. Do I go straight or make a left?" I couldn't tell if these were puns or not; he kept a totally straight face.

He didn't seem surprised when he dropped us off together. "Have a nice night," he said.

"You too, Mike," the movie star said. "I'm sure you'll get ahead in whatever you do."

Dike, straight, head: the world seemed full of sexual references.

I began to obsess about my apartment. In the best of times I am not the neatest person, and this was not the best of times. The spring on the garbage can was broken; I prayed I had pushed down the top. When was the last time I had changed the kitty litter? Had the toothpaste hardened into little blue-green globs on the bottom of the bathroom sink? "I didn't exactly get a chance to clean up," I told her as I unlocked the door.

"Why not?"

"I guess I wasn't expecting to bring anyone back," I laughed embarrassedly.

"But isn't that why you go to the bar, to bring people back?"

"Well, not always." I began to sweat. Was she asking me if I subconsciously wanted to show people what a slob I was? I put on K.D. Lang's *Shadowland*, then went into my office to get copies of my novels. Nosily she followed me in.

"This place is really a mess," she said. "How can you get any work done in here?"

"I haven't been working much lately. I'm 'in-between projects,' I lied, trying to sound Hollywood. I hustled her out of the office. "Would you like a drink or something?"

" 'Something?' " she smiled that smile.

"Jesus Christ." I gave her my squinty-eyed look, then put my arms around her. She didn't slug me. Again I smelled that Clorox smell. I lifted up my mouth, and soon I was running my tongue along those wonderful white teeth. I kept telling myself: I'm kissing her, I've got my tongue in her mouth, my arms are around her back.

"Isn't it a little hot in here?"

She moved away from me and began unbuttoning her blouse. I turned down the dimmer so there was only a faint glow emanating from my low-voltage track. "You've got a nice view," she said, walking over to the window. Her breasts were bare, slightly orange in my light, but whiter near the window. It was odd; I had seen them so often before, not just in movie theaters but in this very room, for long minutes, with the pause button on my VCR turned to "on." I moved towards her, changing the middle-distance shot to a closeup as I sat down on the windowsill in front of her. But the lighting was not as good as in the movie, and when I closed my eyes to put my mouth on her breasts it was the movie and not the real life image I remembered. Almost immediately her nipples got hard, and she began to pant. She tried to pull me to my feet, I think so we could move to the bedroom. But I held her tight, my arms around her thighs, and ran a finger down the crack in the back of her super-tight jeans. I made a mental note to find out their make, so I could buy a similar pair. My mouth still on her, I began to unzip them. They lay around her ankles as she stood there pressed against me, visible to the sky and anyone who might be on the neighboring roofs. I wished somebody were there, to commemorate it with a photograph. Would my friends ever believe me? It did not occur to me I could see her again. She was panting very heavily, so much so I almost wondered if she were putting it on. But why would she do that? She pulled at me again, and I let her lead me to the bedroom. As I slid down the bed I saw the World Trade Center out the window, winking at me with its red light. I was Gatsby, Eugène Rastignac, Norman Mailer, Donald Trump . . . anyone who had ever conquered a city with the sheer force of longing and desire.

Despite her voraciousness she had trouble coming. It was my fault: between memories of her movies, the sultry beauty of the night, the red light of the World Trade Center, I had a hard time concentrating. What I really wanted was to be dancing with her in the most fabulous disco in the world to my very all-time favorite song, say "Heart of Glass" or "Layla." I realized unhappily that the most recent of these was at least ten years old. I had been suspecting for a long time I was no longer hip, but this was the clincher. Not wanting to bore her, I was desperate to come, but of course this only made the possibility of an orgasm recede even further. I did what I always do under such circumstances, which is to tell the person how crazy I am about them.

"Crazy is right," she said. "You don't even like me. I don't even turn you on."

"I'm nervous," I said. "Just think of Woody Allen the first time he kissed Mia Farrow—though I'd much rather be with you than her. I'll marry you if you want. Tomorrow. No, tonight. We'll drive to Maryland, the way Rock Hudson and Doris Day always used to do." At Rock's name we fell silent. "You didn't know him, did you?" I asked.

"I met him once," she said. "At some benefit." I began to remember unpleasant things about Doris too; how when her husband went to that graveyard in the sky, it turned out most of her millions had disappeared with him.

"What kind of people do you hang out with?" I asked.

"Oh. You know. Just people."

"Famous people or not so famous?"

"Both."

"Gay or straight?"

"It depends on what occasion. You try to be discreet."

"Discreet! What about the bar?"

"I'm a human being," she said. "Just like you. Every once in a while this mood comes over me. And the thing is, photographers, for some reason they don't hassle you about stuff like this."

"Why not?"

"Beats me. There's no place in the world I get hassled with less than in there."

"Except by me."

"Except by you," she smiled.

■ ■ ■

She got up and went to the bathroom. I had run out of
toilet bowl cleaner months ago. As I listened to the flush,
then the running of the sink, I thought of what it would
be like to have her here always. I imagined bringing her
to parties, holiday dinners at my parents. Surely a movie
star would excuse the fact I hadn't given them a grandchild.
Then I thought about being part of her world: directors
and agents to look at my scripts, parties that got mentioned
in the newspaper columns, casually eating at restaurants I
now went to only on special occasions.

She came back and sat on the edge of the bed. "I've got
to be going," she said.

"Why?"

"I'm flying to Zihuatanejo in the morning."

"I'll go with you."

"I don't think my lover would like that."

"*No!*" Tears sprang to my eyes. This time, when I pulled
her to me, it was with real passion and a sense of loss. My
skin grew hot and cold and I heard myself panting, almost
too heavily, as she had before. In my head I was embarrassed, but my body didn't care. She was distant but
accommodating as I wrapped myself around her hand.
After I came she lay next to me for a few minutes, then
sat up.

"I really gotta split," she said.

"I *do* love you," I said. It wasn't true, but it could be.

"How sweet." She ruffled my hair. "But you don't even
know me."

"I know you. I've loved you for years. Can I see you
again?" She shook her head. "Because of that stupid lover?"
I asked. She nodded. "How come she didn't go with you
to the bar?"

"She's in California."

"If she lets you be here all alone, she deserves what she gets."

"Sweetheart," she said. *"Please."*

With my open shirt I followed her to the door. I noticed she wasn't carrying my books. I picked them up and handed them to her. "Don't you want these?" I asked.

She laughed. "Sure."

"You'll read them, won't you?" I demanded.

"I'm slow, but I'll read them."

"Let me know if you like them."

"Okay."

"I mean, let me know even if you don't like them." I paused. "Not that anyone ever doesn't like them."

She leaned forward and pecked me on the lips. "It's been fun." She opened the door.

"Should I give you my phone number? So you can reach me."

"Aren't you listed?"

"Wait a sec, I'll walk you downstairs." Before she could say no, I ran into my bedroom and slipped on my jeans, counting on her disinterested politeness to keep her from leaving without me. As we rode down the elevator I prayed someone in the building would be coming home and see us together, but of course nobody did. She immediately found a cab. "If it makes you feel better, I could have loved you too," she said, then kissed me goodbye again. I watched the taxi as it went down the block, in the direction of the tallest building in the city, before turning at the corner. Her last statement should have filled me with bitter regret, but I felt like shouting off the rooftops for joy.

It was almost three, but I had never felt less sleepy in my life. I was torn between going upstairs and telephoning my friends, and tramping along in the still-warm night. I remembered my bike, and decided to walk back to La Donna to retrieve it. On Sheridan Square gay men were walking to and fro in their tight little shorts, holding hands and looking extraordinarily sexy as they headed over to the piers, the Sunday *Times* tucked under their arms. I pictured them in the moonlight reflected over the river, signaling each other in that silent way they had. For a few seconds I actually forgot about the Plague, and envied them.

When I got to La Donna, there were plenty of women still visible through the glass window of the bar, so I walked back inside. Even though it was too late to charge me, I held out my hand with the ink mark stamped on it, in the hope they would remember I had been there earlier, and with whom. I sat down in the same seat I had sat in before and ordered a beer.

"Have a good time?" Judy asked.

"Not bad," I told her, with a giant smile. "She come here a lot?"

"Once or twice a year. Sometimes more."

"Too bad she's got a girlfriend." I sighed a heartfelt sigh, the kind that indicates what-might-have-been.

The bartender looked at me and laughed. "That's what she told you? Don't believe it for a minute."

"Huh?"

"That's her excuse. For trashing out."

" 'Trashing out?' "

"Sure. She comes down here, gets herself picked up, has a little fun, then goes back to her real life. I went home with her once myself."

"You did?" I couldn't believe this. Judy was unattractive and fat, though rather jolly. "But she seemed so . . . *sweet*."

"She *is* sweet. Even sent me a Christmas card once. Care of the bar. Addressed to 'the bartender with red hair.' I guess she didn't remember my name."

"Jesus-fucking-Christ." I took my beer and walked to the jukebox, from where I could survey the back room. I tried to tell myself Judy was lying, but it was no go. So it wasn't my looks, the fact that I was a writer, the poignancy of my bits of self-revelation—simply the fact that I was the first person who had spoken to her this night; probably anyone would have done.

At first I was pissed, then I began to laugh. Hadn't the same impulse occurred to me any number of times? Was it not occurring to me this very minute, as I exchanged glances with a straggly haired brunette I wouldn't have given a thought to had I not been intoxicated with liquor and sex, the aphrodisiac of fame, at quarter to four on a hot summer evening? "I'm a writer," I told her, after I introduced myself.

"No kidding!" she said. "Are you published?" My heart grew wide as her eyes when I told her I was.

night diving

If I were a painter, I would always be trying to get the glint of sun on the leaves in the afternoon, the shadow of the house and trees and the peeling paint on the white wood chair and table and the ants and the sea in the distance, how the blue of the water becomes indistinguishable from that of the sky on certain kinds of afternoons, how sometimes the sky is white and the water gray from the heat, and because the view never ends the painting would never be finished and I would always want it to go on just a little longer. And then I would be missing other things: how sometimes when the sun is extremely hot it feels like a chill, and how it's much harder to get into the water on those kinds of days, perhaps because the difference in temperature between air and water feels so much greater. And that is why I do what I do, which is to paint things in words, so that I can tell you they go onward and outward forever and hope that you'll understand what I mean and fill it in for me.

In this frame of mind, in that kind of head, dealing with such issues—or rather, to escape dealing with such issues—I went diving. It was on a small and poor island in the Caribbean, just beginning to be developed and hard to get to—you flew to the big island then took a two-hour ferry ride—a flat and unattractive island that was good mostly for scuba diving. Flat and unattractive islands that are good mostly for scuba diving tend to be cheaper than beautiful islands with volcanoes and rain forests and old Spanish churches and native shirts to buy in quaint bazaars—which is why I went there. Because it was the off-season, because I was on the cheaper, less fashionable side of the island, because either we had no lovers or spouses or what lovers or spouses we had were not interested in diving, the people in our hotel found ourselves bound together by the kind of camaraderie that, as in the army or in prison, depends more on circumstance than on personality. In the day we went out on the dive boat and at night we ate or walked on the beach. We were the budget vacationers and we didn't have cars; even if we had there was nowhere to go: there were no discos and the food was terrible. Only the fish was fresh and they steamed or baked it without spices. There were plantains and mangoes and a starchy yam-like thing so dry it was almost inedible; that about did it for the growables. Salad seems undreamt-of in such places.

I liked the lostness of it, days in the water, the boat, the sky. I felt most like myself ninety feet beneath the surface.

I had been in an emotional and writing block and only now that I was away was I beginning to remember who I was. I'd throw myself down on the beach after the second dive of the day and sleep, sometimes not even bothering to lie on my towel. The pressure of the water on my body somehow eased the pressure on my mind; I felt totally at peace. Which was not to say I didn't worry about my tank running out of air, or bumping into a shark, or surfacing so quickly I would get the bends or an air embolism, or both. But these thoughts took place not in my ordinary mind but the one to the left of my body, and somehow they did not count. Sometimes recollections of things I had to do, relationships I had to resolve, would float into my mind. Normally I felt I had to do something about these things, make decisions, write lists—if only so as to hold these things in memory—but now I didn't care whether I forgot them or not: I didn't care what happened. This lack of caring, I realized, was one kind of happiness.

Nobody knew who I was, and I didn't know who they were. Things were entirely on the surface. Not only were there no hidden meanings, there was no point to anything except to keep jumping in the water with a tank on my back. This I could do if my ears held up and I didn't get a cold—and my ears held up and I didn't get a cold—and my happiness continued and expanded, the pure happiness of the body rather than the polluted happiness of the mind, and part of the reason I think I was so happy was that I knew it was about to end.

The serpent entered paradise; it always does: the serpent of sex and knowledge. They are one and the same. Behind the perfectly blank surface of my mind, behind the absolute happiness of my pressurized and depressurized body, an image began to intrude. For a day or so I managed to ignore it, but then one night at dinner, when I saw the efforts I was making to seat myself next to Beryl, I realized I was in its thrall.

She was one of the women in our group, a mousyish blonde from the vast plains of Canada. In other circumstances I would not have given her a thought, my glance would have passed right over her in a New York bar—but this was not a bar, these were not other circumstances— she sat at my table three times a day and hung upside down next to me as we peered into caves where fish retreated from our benign hands. Almost any female would have done, but the only other one in our group was a married woman named Carol who lied about her age and flirted with the dive instructor. He did not seem to like her.

Beryl was from Canada, the desert patches of Saskatoon where the wind howled down from the Arctic Circle; when you parked you used an electric heater under the hood to keep the battery from freezing. It got forty degrees below there in the winter and it was the dream of sunshine that got her into a pool week after week with a mask on her face and a tank on her back and a regulator in her mouth to earn a certificate so she could somersault with the sharks and the eels. The tank held the pressurized air but it was the regulator—a hose with a mouthpiece at the end of it which snaked from the tank to your mouth—that delivered it to you at the proper pressure. On land the large metal cans of compressed air bowed our backs but in the greater buoyancy of the water they became weightless, so that we had to put lead on our weight belts to bring us down to the bottom. The regulator was our life line, but I always felt if I could only relax enough, breathe slow enough, I could remove it from my mouth and suck the oxygen out of the water and into my lungs like a fish. Unlike the air that bubbled out of the regulator when you mistakenly tilted it towards the surface you could not see the oxygen in the ocean, but it was there, just like the oxygen you could not see in the air we normally walked in. The deeper you went the more compressed was the oxygen so if you were deep enough the tiniest pinprick of a bubble would contain enough oxygen to keep your heart beating. We were told that if we ran out of air we should rise slowly to the surface, constantly exhaling, following our carbon dioxide bubbles: if our lungs were full, there should be enough oxygen in them, no matter how deep we were, to last us till we got there.

Even when you were not out of air you still had to follow your bubbles to the surface. If you rose faster than your bubbles, the air in your lungs could expand under the lesser pressure and burst a blood vessel in the lungs, causing death within two minutes.

Why a blood vessel in the lungs was so much more important than one you cut in your hand I didn't, and still don't, understand.

The carbon dioxide bubbles you followed to the surface were large and rose rapidly, whereas the oxygen bubbles you could breathe were hidden in the water. Usually when I began to think about ripping off my regulator and becoming a fish and breathing the water I was way down where the water was very blue and the sound of my breathing loud and slow and tortured-sounding in my ears. This was rapture of the deep and that little voice inside my head, the one that almost never shut up, would tell me to head towards the surface. I would do it—with regret—but I would do it. Ten or twenty feet and I would be myself again. Later, on land, I sometimes regretted my docility, my saneness.

Nothing seemed more incongruous to me than Beryl

from Saskatoon getting red in the sun, nothing further from what she seemed to be or rather what my dream of Canadians was, but she said the flatness of the island reminded her in a weird way of home, things stretching out unbroken in all directions to the horizon. She told me Canadians worshiped the sun and that they would drive their vans down to Mexico every winter to camp for months in the Yucatan—not the popular Yucatan of the tourists, but the more deserted, southern part of the state—in campgrounds without electricity or toilets, where you had to drive to town to find a phone. The Canadians who could do this were the ones who worked outdoors: you could not work outdoors in Canada in the winter or you would freeze. Beryl had her own year-round business— servicing office machines—so she could not escape for the long vacation, but like other Canadians she liked the sun.

I was worried she also liked the scuba dive instructor, Jean-Paul. He had black curly hair and that Gallic look of amused superiority. I almost wanted to sleep with him myself, if only to show Beryl and the married woman what I could do.

Beryl was naïve, and I wanted to shock her. She had only slept with two men; my list astounded her.

"Are you talking about men you went out with or men you slept with?" she asked dubiously.

"Men I slept with," I said.

"Do you have a boyfriend now?"

"No. I'm gay."

"What?" Couldn't she hear, or didn't she know what the word meant?

"Gay. Homosexual. I like to sleep with women."

I stared at her. She laughed hysterically. We jumped in the water.

■ ■ ■

We were drinking a beer at a table under the thatched roof of the restaurant before dinner. The sun had disappeared around four, and the wind had picked up. The palms were swaying, there was moisture in the air. It looked a little bit like a 1950s movie, and a little bit like a David Hockney drawing. Normally I hate this kind of weather, but it created a dramatic sense that had been missing in the pleasant sameness of the sunshine. I would not have chosen it but now that it was here, being who I was, I had to play up to it.

The others had gone into town with the dive instructor to pick up some equipment and maybe have a drink at the new bar. If I had not known that Beryl was staying behind, I would have joined them.

"You want a beer?" I asked her when she joined me after her nap. "It's on me."

"No. I'll have a Coke."

"Come on. Live a little."

Reluctantly she accepted a beer. "You were kidding," she asked, "before?"

"Before what?" Of course I knew what she was referring to.

"About liking women?"

"Of course not."

"I mean, not about liking women—we all like women—but you know, in that way."

"I like women *in that way*, Beryl." In a theatrical, over-dramatized fashion I made myself move my eyes from her face to her cleavage, as if I were a guy, a person who cared about breasts.

"Stop it," she said. "It's not funny."

"All right." I looked away. She calmed down a little.

I couldn't help it, I reached out as if to grab her breasts. She jumped up clutching her beer to her chest.

"Come on," I said. "I'm just kidding."

She moved as far away from me at the table as she could. "I don't trust you," she said.

"Why not?"

"You've got a sick sense of humor. I don't even believe you're a . . . what you said you were. If you were like you said you were, you couldn't have made love with all those guys."

"We didn't make love, Beryl, we *fucked*. And now I *fuck* women. Lots of them."

She narrowed her eyes as if looking at a painting, or at a distance over water in the sun. "I've never met someone like you before."

"I *am* special," I said.

"I mean, like you sexually. There are no homosexuals in Saskatoon."

It was my turn to laugh. "You've met them," I said. "You just didn't know it."

Then the others returned, drunk and boisterous, and it was time to eat.

After dinner Carol took Beryl off to her room. I stayed at the restaurant with the divers and the scuba dive instructor, who were continuing their predinner party with tequila and lime. "Are you really gay?" asked Josh.

"Sure."

"But you've fucked guys too?"

"Yeah. You mean you haven't?" I asked innocently.

"Are you kidding?"

"Why haven't you?"

"Let a guy stick his dick up my butt, you got to be kidding. That's disgusting!"

"That's kind of how I feel about it too," I said. "And I'll bet my vagina's a lot cleaner than your ass!"

Even the scuba dive instructor had to laugh.

The guys began to ask me what I thought of the women around the hotel: Beryl, Carol, the mulatta who ran the place, and the young girl who cleaned our rooms. "The young girl's hot," I said, "but I think Carol's got the best bod."

"She's got those stretch marks though."

"Even so."

"I thought Beryl was more your type," said the scuba dive instructor.

"A little old-fashioned, but I wouldn't kick her out of bed. What about you?"

He shrugged and refused to answer.

We began to make up limericks, dirty limericks about each of us. Mine went:

> There was a young lass from Manhattan
> Whose sheets were not made of satin
>   Her preference was women
>   The kind she could come in
> Doing acts unheard of in Latin.

Beryl and Carol rejoined us. Carol had been giving Beryl what she called a French manicure on her toes.

"Very pretty," I said. I meant it, though I also hated it. It reminded me of camp, where the girls had spent all their time curling their hair for the boys when what I was really interested in was playing softball.

"I could do it for you, too, if you want," Carol offered.

"Watch out for her," warned Jeff. "She likes your tits."

We began to recite our limericks for them:

An old married woman with gall
Decided she'd like to go AWOL
    She never felt more alive
    Then when deep on a dive
Where they said she had quite a ball.

There was a young female Canadian
Who considered herself quite a maiden
    She couldn't stand sex
    Even with her ex
To this day she's never been laid in.

Carol laughed, but Beryl looked disgusted. It was our act to try to gross her out; it was her act to be grossed out. The scuba dive instructor silently watched us. I imagined his contempt for us—all the tourists who spent time and money to do things he got paid to do.

Almost in tears, Beryl left. I watched the dive instructor follow her with his eyes. Although I knew people would talk, I ran off after her.

"Is something the matter?" I asked. Only it came out: "Ish shomething the matter?"

"No."

"There ish. I can tell."

"Leave me alone," she said. "You're drunk." She ran into her little bungalow and shut the door. I banged on it but she would not let me in. The light came on and through the window I watched her throw herself on the bed. She was sobbing. She looked up and saw me watching her, so she got up and shut the wooden shutters in my face. I waited a while, then knocked on the door again. When there was no response, I headed back to the restaurant.

A short distance from our group, I leaned against the bar, watching them. Carol was teasing the scuba dive instructor about his virility. She was nearly as drunk as I was. She said women were better lovers than men because they could fuck even when they were drunk. She asked the scuba dive instructor if he was drunk. Did he agree or disagree with her theory?

Listening to this, I grew depressed. I imagined the expression in my eyes was the same as Beryl's listening to our limericks. I tried to make it the same as Beryl's, so that I would become worthy of her—worthy of her uptightness.

All of a sudden Carol turned to me. I hadn't realized she had known I was standing there. "What's the matter with you?" she demanded. "Do you have a stick up your ass or what?"

Beryl began to get nervous around me. If my leg brushed hers on the dive boat or at the table she'd move away. Of course this prompted me to push my leg harder against hers, very obviously, in a kind of parody of desire. I realized I wasn't so much trying to arouse her as irritate her. But perhaps this was my way of arousing her. I told myself that this apparent aversion was a compliment. She was attracted to me and was trying to deny it. It had been this way with other women, although it did not necessarily lead to great success. I told myself I didn't care, it was all a game—something to add piquancy to the days and while away the nights. It was a game because I wouldn't have bothered with Beryl in New York. She was too much trouble and she was not attractive enough.

And yet I did not feel it was a game. It seemed as if everything depended on it: the success of my trip, my future sexual life, even my writing. The water had begun freeing me from my block. I did not want a human being to fuck it up.

After dinner the next night Beryl immediately went off to her bungalow. As usual, Carol began coming on to the scuba instructor. I couldn't stand it any longer, and I walked down the beach by myself. I lay on a hammock gazing at the water, thinking how happy I had been a few days before and how unhappy I was now, now that the serpent of desire had entered my life and I had lost the innocent forms of happiness.

The scuba dive instructor appeared. He was walking alone. I asked him if he wanted to smoke a joint with me, but he said no, he was busy.

The next day there was a storm in the afternoon, and we couldn't go out on our afternoon dive. Jeff and I were driving into town to check out the market, and I asked Beryl if she wanted to come with us.

"No thanks," she said.

"What're you going to do all by yourself?" I asked. "Don't you want some company?" I put my arm around her neck, but she darted away.

"I don't believe you're gay at all," she said.

"What?"

"You asked Jean-Paul if he wanted to smoke a joint with you last night."

I shrugged. My motives in regard to the dive instructor were ambiguous—even to myself. Certainly I wanted to keep him away from Beryl. He had not been interested in me, so I could not tell whether or not I would have slept with him.

. . .

Beryl and I were buddies on the next day's first dive. Because of the way the nitrogen got absorbed and released by one's body, the first dive was always deeper than the second. I liked deep dives for the macho power of them, the eerie blueness of the water, the silence that was only made more profound by the rasping of my breath or the occasional clunk of the regulator valve against the tank; I liked the shallow dives because we used up air less quickly and could stay down longer, because there was enough light to display the fish in their full spectrum of colors, because you didn't have to hover ten or twenty feet beneath the surface waiting to rid your body of excess nitrogen before climbing back onto the boat.

Beryl and I followed the line of the anchor down to the ocean floor. There were six or seven of us; like baby ducks we swam after the dive instructor as he guided us around the reef. When there was an extra person he had a buddy—usually the worst diver; otherwise he moved from group to group, making sure we stayed with our buddies, had enough air, avoided touching fire coral, etc. Sometimes he would stop at a reef or in front of a cave to point something out, and you could see sets of fins moving up and down in a slow flutter kick after him. When we saw what he wanted us to we would nod our heads and make a circle with our thumb and forefinger, then move aside for the other divers. If we missed it we would shake our heads and put our arms up in a gesture of exasperation, and he would glide back to try and point it out: a lobster, a moray, a giant urchin. On occasion he would shine his flashlight on the plastic-sealed pages of his waterproof book so that we could know—or at least give a name to—what we had seen. Sometimes it seemed that I was seeing everything there was to see and yet I saw nothing, I didn't know what was special. Would a New Guinea tribesman brought to Europe know that a television was ordinary and the Parthenon extraordinary?

When something was dangerous the dive instructor would hold up his hand like a policeman, warning us to stop. Once he grabbed my fin as I was chasing a long, thin fish which had slithered past me like a snake. On the surface he told me it was a moray eel; I would have been seriously hurt if it had bitten me. Another time he pointed to what looked like a rock on the ocean floor. I would have swum over to it if he had not made a fist for danger; he told me later it was the fatal stonefish. The next day when I was hovering near him clearing my mask he motioned me towards him. We were on a deep dive and it took me a moment to see the fat black figure against the blue. It did not have jagged fins but I could tell instantly it was a shark: game fish were sleek and beautiful in their shiny coats of many colors, whereas the predators—sharks and barracuda—were fat and unreflective in the most boring shades of white, black, gray. Another way to put it was that the game fish were like the women of Bali or India in their colorful robes, whereas the predators were dressed like typical New Yorkers at a party. I stared at it a while, this fat ugly dark-gray thing, then with a flip of its tail it was gone. You could not follow it with your eyes or even your body as you could the other fish; it just disappeared.

On the surface I asked Jean-Paul why he had motioned me to the shark, when he was so careful to make sure we avoided the other dangers.

He laughed. "A shark can go eighty miles an hour. If he decided to go after you, do you really think you could avoid him?"

On the afternoon dive he stuck his flashlight inside a cave. Dutifully we tried to see what he wanted us to. Beryl and I were last. I peered into the cave, shook my head and shrugged my shoulders, then moved aside for her. We were upside down. I held on to the top of the cave with my hands so the current would not drag me away, and she drifted over next to me. As she peered into the cave, her long blondish hair swirled through the water. A fish came out of the cave and swam through it. It was an ordinary fish, not what we were peering in the cave to see. Finally her head came up, and she shrugged her shoulders too.

We let go of the wall of the cave. She was about to move forward to join the others when I held up my hand so she would stop, then I took my regulator out of my mouth, holding it mouthpiece downwards so no bubbles could escape. She pointed to my tank and then her mouth, to ask if I were out of air. I shook my head but she came towards me anyway. She put her left hand on my right shoulder the way you were supposed to and took the regulator out of her mouth and offered it to me.

We were face to face, ninety feet under. Sunlight slanted down in discrete rays as through a window high up on the wall in a gothic church. It was amazingly quiet and still, as holy as church, a church I didn't believe in; but I began to feel I could maybe get to believe in it if only I could relax enough, breathe slowly enough, learn the mysteries of air—which was the hidden secret of fish, the way they found air where it did not seem to exist. If I could find air where it did not exist would I not live forever too? This was another kind of happiness that went beyond the non-caring of the mind and the simple pleasures of the body to the very center of my being, and I felt at that moment it was the best, the truest, the most complete of all. Beryl was looking at me strangely, and her hand slipped, and the hose that snaked from the tank to her hand was facing upwards, its noisy bubbling disturbing my holy and quiet cathedral. She grabbed it and put it in her mouth, exhaled the water from it, then bubbles flew out of her too. They were large bubbles, much larger bubbles than the ones I knew were hidden in the water all around me, and they were made not of air but of carbon dioxide. No matter how much smarter or quieter I was, no matter how much attention I paid, I could not live off them.

I ripped the regulator out of her mouth. She looked frightened. I pulled her towards me and kissed her. This was yet another kind of happiness, the kind that came from a human being—that is, the idea of a human being whom you desired and who hopefully desired you in return.

It was a stupid kiss. You can't feel anything underwater. The saliva was there but it was so mingled with salt and water you could only sense rather than taste its slight gluey-ness. Being surrounded by wetness, the wetness itself wasn't interesting. I liked the idea of it, however.

She pushed me away, stuck her regulator back in her mouth; then, ignoring all the rules of underwater safety, swam away from me, her buddy.

When she was maybe twenty feet away she stopped and turned. No doubt she was wondering whether I had put my regulator back in my mouth. She hovered there like a mutant water mammal: half game fish with her blond hair and turquoise snorkel and mask and yellow buoyancy compensator device covering her striped swimsuit like a jacket, half predator like the sharks with her black fins and gray tank and weights. But the rapture of the deep had gone away from me and I knew I could breathe only in the normal, nonmysterious way—through my regulator, not the water: the sane way of humans rather than the crazy one of fish.

I flutter-kicked towards her and we joined the others. They had been looking for us, and the dive instructor signaled to ask if we were okay. I was relieved when Beryl held her thumb and forefinger together in a closed circle.

I was distracted the rest of the dive, fantasizing what would happen when we got back to the surface. I kept telling myself to pay attention—I was spending lots of money to be here—but these imagined scenes were more vivid than the fish. For me, imagined scenes were always more real than real ones, even when, as in sex, the imagined scene was the same I would have seen if only I had opened my eyes. I envisioned the boat: the guys teasing me about making a pass, my feeling macho about it—a bit of a pig— Beryl glaring at me, and the scuba instructor getting even by forbidding me to go on the night dive he had scheduled for the following night.

Night dives are rare. Instructors hate to lead them. You have to use flashlights and sometimes people—often the ones you'd least expect—get freaked out.

I made sure to climb onto the boat before Beryl. The dive instructor lifted the backpack with its tank off her back and she began taking off her weight belt and BCD. This vacation was her first time in open water and she did not have a wet suit; as soon as her gear was off she slipped on a sweatshirt. She always did this, and it always looked funny, her shivering in the eighty-degree air with a sweat-shirt on her back. I waited for her to open her mouth. I still had not come up with a foolproof explanation for my behavior, one that would exonerate me completely and yet not get her into trouble either—for I was still hoping I could get her to like me.

"What happened to you?" asked the scuba dive instructor. "It's dangerous to lose contact like that."

Beryl looked at me. I waited for the blow. "The regulator got tangled when we were upside down," she said. "It was nothing, really."

"It's not nothing on a night dive."

I gave Beryl my biggest crocodile smile, both to thank her and apologize. She looked away, as if to tell me she was doing this not for me but for herself. I tried to tell myself it was because she liked me, but just as likely it was because she didn't want to be teased by the guys, or have the scuba instructor think I knew her well enough to attempt something like that.

I realized there had been nothing to worry about. I had not counted sufficiently on her conventionality, her sanity.

"Leave me alone," she said that night before dinner when I tried to apologize. "I think you're sick."

"Come on, Beryl," I said. "Rapture of the deep."

"Bull—" She couldn't bring herself to say "bullshit." "You were alone with me and you tried to take advantage of me."

"Take advantage of you. Like I'm going to rape you ninety feet down." But I wasn't sure about the rapture of the deep either; perhaps I had used it, the way others use alcohol, to allow myself to do something my normal mind wouldn't—or perhaps, even more oddly, as a way to prove I really was gay, that I hadn't been coming on to the scuba dive instructor like Carol or Beryl or any of the other women at the hotel. In any case, I understood Beryl's conventionality because I shared it: it was our characters that were different, not our hearts. I was tougher than her, because I forced myself to overcome my conventional scruples; on the other hand, she was more honest, less of a hypocrite, than me. I could not decide which of these virtues was the more admirable.

"Who knows what's on your sick mind?" she said.

She was such a parody I could not get angry at her.

"Even shrinks don't call it sick anymore."

"Well, it *is* sick!"

"Keep it down," I said. Because she had refused to be alone with me, we were standing less than thirty feet away from the rest of the group. She had not talked to me since the dive, and everyone could tell something was up. For a while I had liked this—being at the center of a slightly shocked attention in a way that could never happen in New York—but I was beginning to feel like a clown.

"It was your idea to talk, not mine."

"It's too small a group to have shit going on," I said.

"Then keep out of my way."

She walked away. Was I crazy, or were the guys laughing at me? Because I was scared to join them, I forced myself to. "I'll have what you're having," I said. They were drinking the tall island drink—part rum, part coconut, part something else.

Jeff snickered. "Yeah, I bet you wish you were having what I'm having."

"Yeah, Jeff, what are you having?"

He smirked. "Maybe I put it wrong. Maybe I should have said, I bet you wish you had what I have." He ran his hand suggestively over the front of his bathing suit. Only Carol didn't laugh. I tried to excuse it on the grounds he was drunk, but I knew the truth was that the drunkenness permitted him to say what he really felt.

"This hand, Jeff," I said, turning it in the air this way and that as if it were a model on a runway, "can do stuff you've never dreamt of, and then some."

"Yeah, Jeff, her little pinkie is probably the size of your dick."

"I'd check it out," I said, "if only I had a magnifying glass."

It was a joke I had used a million times before, but everybody laughed.

After dinner I suddenly realized that both the scuba dive instructor and Beryl had disappeared. I took my drink and headed down the beach. I sat sideways in the hammock, idly pushing my foot against the sand. A few stars were up, but mostly the sky was a deep lavender gray.

Carol joined me. I made room for her on the hammock. "Men are pigs," she said.

"It's you who like them, not me."

"Well, what else can you do?"

"There's women," I said.

"Thanks but no thanks. I like dick."

I had deliberately spoken in a nonsexy way, but of course she would think I was making a pass at her. Women who slept with men always acted as if you were making a pass at them. They set you up with comments and then, when you stated the obvious, pretended you had been coming on to them all along. You could not tell them you were not, because that was cruel and they would accuse you of being defensive. They had a belief they were irresistible—not necessarily (or at least any longer) to men, but to women with preferences like mine. They seemed to believe that if they went so far as to indicate they might be interested in you, it was your obligation not to turn them down—as years ago, when sex came with greater difficulty than it does now, it might have been a man's obligation not to turn them down. It was as if women like me were like men years ago, desperate enough to accept anything. Sometimes this was true, but it irked me that these other women always acted like they weren't desperate or willing to accept anything themselves—even when this clearly wasn't true.

It was too generalized to be personally insulting, but it was insulting nonetheless. Because I liked women who had never slept with women it was somewhat true of me, but it was less true of other women I knew who liked to sleep with women. They were more intelligent than me; the last thing they wanted was to get involved with someone who might be terrible in bed, or be filled with recriminations, or leave them for the first guy to come along. It always made me wonder what women who generally or always slept with men thought bars for women like me were like: places where you could sleep with whoever you wanted because you were such a pervert that there wasn't anything in the world you wouldn't do, and no one in the room you wouldn't do it with? I wondered if they thought we were like the men who were like us, fucking standing up in the back rooms of bars, the only lights those of red cigarette tips and yellow flashes from lighters, the only sounds those of zippers being pulled up and down, moans and slaps and the suck of things moving in and out of holes that perhaps were not meant to be entered. I used to hate and envy and have contempt for men for just this reason. I thought they were pigs and I wanted to be like them and I hated myself for wanting to be like them. Now that the Plague has come this jealousy seems laden with irony, a moral lesson. But there are no lessons, just interpretations that are both consistent with the facts and please us.

"I like pussy," I said.

We listened to the ocean hitting the reef. The wind and currents were stronger here, and the better diving hotels were on the other side of the island.

"Actually, I hate that word," I said. "I don't know why I used it."

"I don't like dick either."

This was an ambiguous statement. I offered her my drink. The moon had risen; through the clouds it threw a path of light on the water, almost a parody of a certain kind of painting. "You think Beryl and the scuba dive instructor are getting it on?" I asked.

"I would say so," she said. "If they did last night and the night before, why wouldn't they now?"

"Oh." If I considered myself so smart, how come I hadn't known this?

"You've got a thing for her, don't you?"

"In a way. Just for here. Not back home."

"I'd go for him back home. In a minute."

"He is pretty cute," I said.

"I don't know what he sees in her." What she really meant was: I don't know why he prefers her to me.

But the thing was, she did know. Beryl was younger and untouched; it was her innocence—the only wisdom experience cannot teach you—that turned the dive instructor on.

We stood up and headed back. I walked on the wet sand next to the water. I rolled my pants up so they wouldn't get wet, but they did. They picked up sand and it felt more disgusting than it should have, the way shit does in one's pants—though of course this was not as bad.

We stopped in front of Carol's hut. "You could come in for a drink, you know."

She was older than me, a little crass, a little weathered, but in a boozy country-club way I knew she would be considered attractive. That is, if I were someone else she would be attractive.

It was a night I didn't mind being somebody else. "All right," I said.

We were lying on her bed in the dark. The moon had risen and it came in, white and ghostly, through the bars of the wooden shutters onto the wall. The ceiling fan rotated. It felt like a dream, the dream of an island.

"You've slept with women before, haven't you?" I asked her later. You can tell: she was not surprised enough by certain things, she didn't evince enough guilt or wonder, she didn't ritually imitate me, the way women who've never slept with women always do.

"Only when I was drunk."

"You said you hadn't."

"I was drunk. It was just a one-time thing. It didn't count."

"Are you drunk now?" I asked.

"Aren't I always, this time of night?"

There were two approaches: to leave now, so that nobody would know, or to swagger out of her bungalow in the morning.

I felt pity for her, as I often do for people I sleep with and don't really like. When she pulled me to her breast so I could suck on it, I realized she probably felt the same way about me.

■ ■ ■

There was only one dive the next day, because we were going out at night. Usually Beryl was my buddy, but this time the scuba dive instructor paired me with Jeff. Jeff carried a camera, and he was having trouble with his flash, so we lagged behind the others. Beryl was with Jean-Paul, and they swam back searching for us. They were holding hands. It meant nothing—diving buddies often hold hands—but I knew it was everything.

Normally we didn't drink at lunch, but because we weren't diving until night the guys started on the beer. It was hot and windless and sticky and on a day like this it made them nasty.

"Lot of action around here last night," Josh said to Jeff.

"Yeah, those springs were really humming." They stared at me and Beryl. Carol had skipped lunch, saying she had a headache.

Jean-Paul looked at them with disgust, then asked Beryl if she wanted to take a walk down the beach. Both the guys and I stared angrily after them. I realized why we were all so upset: it was a violation of our little community, a statement that some were more important than others. Under water, where our lives were in a sense in the dive instructor's hands, you did not want to be considered less important than anybody else.

It occurred to me the reference to bedsprings might have been about me as well, though up till then I had assumed they didn't know. Carol had me leave her bungalow around six, and we had scarcely spoken on the morning dive. She was the worst diver—more experienced but less in control than Beryl—and got paired either with the scuba instructor or with Josh.

"Yeah, lots of action around here," said Jeff pointedly to me.

"Jealous?" I asked.

"Some people will sleep with anything," he said.

I went alone with a book and a towel to the beach. The air was so hot it was gray, and even when the sun disappeared behind the clouds it made no difference. I tried to cool myself off by going into the water, but it didn't do any good. No matter what I did I was uncomfortable. I tried to read in a hammock, but I could not concentrate. When I shut my eyes the sun made spots on them—not pretty spots, as sometimes happened, but silver-gray ones. They swam in front of the landscape for a few seconds when I opened my eyes. In spite of the dive and the swimming I could still smell Carol on my hand. Although I was tired I could not fall asleep and my mind was racing, partly about Carol, who seemed to be avoiding me, but mostly about Beryl, off with the scuba dive instructor. I could not tell if I actually cared, or if it was the memory of caring. I felt like a fool, but I wasn't sure whether this was due to Beryl, or Carol, or the guys.

Around three Carol emerged from her bungalow. She asked me if I wanted to take a walk.

"Aren't you hungry?" I asked.

"I took a sandwich in from the kitchen."

We bought two beers and walked down the beach beyond the point, where nobody could see us, then we took off our suits and went into the slate-colored water. It was very hot but the sun was not out and the water felt creepy, both hot and cold at once, so I quickly got out.

I lay down naked on the sand. The sand stuck to my hair and my arms and legs, but for some reason I did not find it as disgusting as when it had stuck to my pants. I even rolled onto my stomach, so my entire body was coated. The suntan oil I was using helped make it stick to my body.

"You look like a coconut," Carol said when she sat down next to me on her towel. She was too careful of her manicure and hair to give in to such impulses as mine.

"I smell like a coconut," I said. She leaned over as if to smell me, but of course it was a pretext to kiss me. I kissed her back. Her breath smelled of beer. To escape her, I ran into the water. Diving had made me lazy, so for a long time I just floated on my back, my lids closed. I could feel the hazy sun burning me, or maybe it was the salt. By keeping my lungs almost totally full of air, I managed to stretch and even do a little yoga, then I told myself to swim.

Normally my body does what I tell it to, but this time it didn't want to. Swimming seemed boring and pointless, so I headed to shore.

"You want to go back and take a siesta?" Carol asked.

"No."

"Is something the matter?"

"I don't like having sex during the day."

When we came back the guys looked at us as if we had been fucking. By men's standards we had been gone a fairly long time—but not by women's. A joke was on the tip of my tongue, but it was so predictable—both the joke and the imagined reaction—that I skipped it.

■   ■   ■

We assembled with our gear at around nine in front of the dive boat. Again Jeff was my buddy, Josh was with Carol, the dive instructor was with Beryl.

In addition to the usual equipment, we had flashlights attached to our wrists. We were to flash them on and off rapidly as a signal if we got into trouble. But Jean-Paul assured us there was nothing to worry about: a lantern would be attached to the bottom of the anchor line in case we got lost, but anyway it was impossible to get lost, because it was easier to see a person holding a light at night than it was to spot them amidst the fish and coral during the day. Although there was nothing to be frightened of people sometimes did get scared, and if by chance we did we shouldn't be embarrassed: just signal your buddy, then go to the anchor line and tug on it so the guy on the boat would know you were coming to the surface.

"What about sharks?" I asked. I had always heard how it was dangerous to swim at night because of the sharks.

"You think they're not there during the day?"

The ocean looked like oily ink, but as soon as I jumped in I felt fine. I had expected a shock, but the water was no colder than the air, which made it oddly comforting. It was dark, but no more so than on land. With our glowing lights we were like coal miners in a cave. We flashed to each other that we were okay, then began to let the air out of our buoyancy compensator devices as we drifted slowly down.

Our body movements disturbed the tiny phosphorescent fish, and the water was filled with little pinpricks of light. These looked like stars, and I imagined I was a paratrooper on a night drop.

When we reached the bottom we exhaled air into our BCDs until we could hover with our fins just touching the sand, rising slightly as we inhaled and sinking slightly as

we exhaled. The instructor swam over to the anchor line
and attached the lantern to it. Overhead you could see a
huge black shadow, the bottom of the boat.

The instructor took Beryl's hand, and signaled us to
follow him.

Floating miners, parachutists in free fall, we followed
his bobbing light. Fish materialized out of the dark into
our lights, astonishing us with their colors, then immediately disappeared. The arc my flashlight illuminated was
small, and I was worried about the fish I could not see: I
kept turning around to look for sharks. But all I ever saw
were small schools of yellow, violet, or rainbow-colored
fish. Because they did not know we were there until we
were in their midst they were much closer to us than
during the day. I shut my flashlight off, and soon I could
feel them brushing against my body. Unlike the human
body, they were totally clean and they did not smell.

Jeff was tugging my arm. I thought he was angry at me
for turning off the flashlight, but he pointed with his
thumb to the surface. I signaled to ask him whether he
was okay and if he had enough air. He nodded, then
pointed again to the surface. I flashed my light at Josh
and Carol, and they waited with me as we watched Jeff
swim towards the anchor line. He tugged on it, and we
saw another light flash, from the man on the boat. We saw
Jeff's light floating slowly up through the water to the
surface.

Carol tilted her head and pointed with her thumb at
Jeff, the way you do when you mime a question. I shrugged
my shoulders, then made a circle with the forefinger of
my right hand in the vicinity of my right temple. I didn't
know why, but Jeff must have gotten freaked. Although I
was a far less experienced diver than Jeff I realized I was

not scared at all, much less so than I was during the day. For once I wasn't even thinking about running out of air. Sharks might be out there, but if they came close enough for me to see them it would only be for half a second.

I extended my arms and hung, moving just slightly upwards or downwards when I breathed, then I somersaulted upside down. There was no particular reason to do this, other than the simple joy of being a weightless acrobat—a weightless acrobat in an alien world where there was no air save that which you carried on your back, beneath a dark and alien sky that glowed with stars which were the emissions of photons from millions of excited microscopic fish, a hop, skip and a jump from the ship that would bring me safely home.

I was an astronaut and I trusted my ship to bring me back to shore. I trusted my ship and my tank and even my scuba dive instructor, who had betrayed me, and yet, in a temporary but profound sense, I didn't care. The pressure of the water on my body was again managing to ease the pressure on my mind, and I felt totally at peace. It was the happiness of the body rather than the polluted happiness of the mind, and it had absolutely nothing to do with other people or the complicated relations between them we call sex. It was the pure and simple happiness I had felt when I first came to the island, and I realized once again it was the best.

I turned and caught Carol doing a somersault. She was trying to imitate my bliss—or maybe just my actions. It was my bliss and not hers, but when she landed in front of me I let her take the regulator out of my mouth and kiss me. I had told her what I had done to Beryl, and no doubt she was imitating that too. It would ruin my pure and simple happiness, but it is the essence of pure and simple happiness to be ruined by human beings. Then she reached out her hand and forced it inside my suit. It was fun, in an anecdotal sort of way, but it certainly had nothing to do with rapture of the deep.

butch

She was so ugly I found her attractive, though of course I didn't want anybody to see me with her. When I left the bar I made her walk several feet behind me, like Chinese women used to do. I told her it was because I didn't want anybody to see me with a woman, but really it was just her—with her crewcut, what would people think? This was long before punk had made short hair respectable. Even inside my building I made her walk a flight behind me up the stairs. I was poor then, and lived in a walk-up on the Bowery. And yet I was not unhappy, for I lived entirely for love. Much of the city did then, though it never will again.

I put on a record, took out two beers and a joint, turned

down the lights, and sat next to her on the couch. I felt relaxed, as I always do with someone less attractive than me, since then it's up to them to initiate sex. I would never have walked over to anybody who looked like her at the bar. And yet as I stared at her pale, soft skin, her close-cropped head, my pants got wet: amazing. A wave of total peace washed over me and I shut my eyes. The ball was not in my court. Whatever happened, happened. I didn't choose it and it was not my fault.

She began to tell me about her life. She had grown up in some small town upstate, the kind of dreary place one might look back at with pleasure, but would yearn to escape from at the time. But even in retrospect there was no pleasure for her, because her father had caught her humping her girlfriend on a sleepover date when she was sixteen and beat her up. A year later he caught them again and threw her out of the house. The girlfriend left her to marry some guy, so she moved to New York, where there were other people like her. It was during one of the lulls in the East Village, and she quickly found a share in a four-room walk-up between First and A. The normal thing for someone like her to have done would have been to become a waitress, but she wasn't attractive enough, so she took this job her roommate found her in a T-shirt factory. They were lovers, though Diane was fat, unattractive, a real cunt. All day long they hammered stuff on T-shirts— shiny little round things that made patterns. It was lower-class, blue-collar, real boring, back in those days before the Sony Walkman. That is, it was boring for Laura to live it, but not for me to listen to it. Everyone I knew was a struggling writer, painter, or some other arty type, so hearing her talk about something other than her foiled ambitions was refreshing.

She was supposed to be at work by eight in the morning,

but she was a night person and often was late. She'd pick up a coffee and bagel and bring it into the factory. Nobody cared, everybody was in their own world. She had gotten to be friends with some of them, but Diane was jealous of anything that moved. Lately they hadn't been getting on so well; that was why she was with me now, though if Diane found out she would kill her. If Diane had walked into Bonnie and Clyde's and seen us talking, she would have beaten Laura up—and maybe me too. But luckily she hung out at Gianni's, where the serious bulldykes went, the ones who were into cross-dressing. At least that's what they used to call it, before the style seeped into the upper classes and got renamed the "androgynous look." Most of the time Diane was on the wagon, but when she got drunk she went absolutely crazy. She would push Laura up against the wall, and throw words like "slut," "bitch," "cocksucking cunt" at her. Then she would slap her. Laura was thin and softspoken, with tiny, birdlike bones, and I could see the pleasure one could have in terrorizing her. Once Diane punched Laura in the face and Laura had a black eye and didn't go to work for almost a week. She made up some story but everybody knew all about it anyway; they always did. Laura would tell Diane that Diane didn't love her, that Diane just wanted to control somebody. But whenever Laura threatened to move out, Diane would threaten to commit suicide, and Laura would end up staying.

"Why did you sleep with her in the first place if she's so horrible?" I asked lazily. But I knew the answer: it was similar to the reason why I was with her tonight, though somebody tall and blond and beautiful was probably lying sleepless now because of me.

"Oh, she's not so bad," said Laura.

The record was done. I thought about getting up and turning it over, but I didn't, then the silence became interesting. I was spacey from the marijuana, and I realized how tired I was of being even a little bit in charge. Of anything. It began to seem more disruptive of the mood to put on music than just let the silence be—though bits of songs played in my head like a movie soundtrack. I realized how rarely I was with another person without some kind of music in the background. I wondered if Laura was playing something in her head too. I cleared my throat to speak, but I stopped. The silence grew more and more awkward, but then, this very awkwardness should compel her to do something.

As I waited I began imagining Laura and Diane together in bed: a fat bulldyke and a water-pale wisp. The relationship was mysterious, incomprehensible, but what relationship wasn't? The tall blond woman who waited for me—my "official" girlfriend—who was she and what did it mean when she said she loved me? What could it possibly mean when I told her I loved her? What relationship did the person I thought I was have with the one sitting here on the couch, my pants wet at the idea of having sex with someone I kept telling myself disgusted me. Was it that I secretly liked her and was embarrassed by my attraction, or was it the disgust itself I liked? Did Laura put up with the fear and beatings because she liked Diane, or was it the fear and beatings that she liked?

"What are you thinking?" she asked.

"Oh, nothing." I waited a while. "Actually, I was thinking about Diane. Whether she'll punch you out when you go home."

"Does it turn you on to think about that?"

"Maybe."

Her hand slipped inside my blouse and touched my nipples. They were erect. Her hands were cold. I heard myself breathing fast, and the utter shamelessness of this—

the person I was breathing fast for—only made me breathe even faster. Had I ever been more turned on? And yet, she was scarcely doing anything, barely circling the tips of my nipple with her finger. Why couldn't she put her mouth there? My body strained towards her as in a bad porno movie. She shoved her hand inside my closed jeans, though because of the tightness of the jeans she couldn't get very far—maybe a little south of the belly button. I twisted to meet her fingers, to move my pubic hairs a little more towards her. I yearned for her to undo my belt, unsnap the snap, pull down the zipper, slide her pale white fingers inside my underpants, spread my legs, drive me crazy with her icy touch. But no, she continued this lazy circling of her finger. Gradually the yearning turned to anger, that she was dawdling, torturing me by this slow tease. And yet, oddly, the angrier I got, the more my respect for her grew.

Finally she put her mouth on my nipple, undid my belt, unzipped my jeans, and slipped her hand inside my underpants. Even then, she didn't shove her fingers straight in, but kept tweaking my pubic hairs, somehow managing to avoid both my clitoris and vagina. The bottom of my body bucked in a way that was at least partly nonvolitional. Her arm pressed down on my pubic bone and I felt like I couldn't move (though of course I could).

"God, you're wet," she said.

At last she pushed her fingers inside my vagina and crawled on top of me, so that the weight of her body was on the arm that was inside me. Whereas before she had been gentle, now she became incredibly rough, jerking her arm back and forth very quickly. I was so wet it didn't hurt. "I bet I could get my whole hand inside," she said, as if in a question.

"Okay," I whispered. At that moment there was nothing

I wouldn't have let her do (though of course there was).

She cupped her fingers, trying to get her hand inside. It was as if I hadn't felt her before, as if my skin had been numb to individual sensations, that I'd been this wet tunnel down which something smooth had been shoved. But now I could differentiate her various fingers. "Three," then "four," she counted out loud. She had to struggle to get this last one in, and so did I. "Am I hurting you?" she asked.

"That's okay."

"If I'm hurting you I'll stop." She started to withdraw her hand. My body sucked after it.

"It feels good," I had to whisper.

"Oh." Was I imagining the triumph in her voice? In any case, she spread me wide, as if she were about to give me a D and C, then I felt her knuckles.

This really hurt, in a way that was hard to tell whether it was pleasurable or not. The tips of my nipples were no longer erect, and the wetness seemed not a response to some unfulfilled yearning but a reflex no more interesting than the turning on of a faucet. And yet I was pushing my legs as far apart as possible. I moaned when she put her teeth around my nipple. "You're very sweet," she told me.

I have always felt this to be true, though very few people have recognized it as such. With my nipple still in her mouth she pushed my jeans down so they encircled my ankles. I was sweating and messy. She was much cooler than me, almost clinical as she proceeded, which not only aroused me but made me like her better. Somehow things were more in balance than earlier in the evening. I wished she had brought a camera with her so we could have taken pictures of me masturbating to the sight of her naked body—and ever after I could torture myself over what she had done with them.

Abruptly she pulled out her hand, then I heard her stand up. I kept my eyes shut, wondering what she was doing, if she was going to search up some strange toy in her pocketbook. I heard her walk away, then behind my lids I saw, or perhaps felt, the warmer glow which I pretended was sun, but which was really a distant light in my apartment. I heard the toilet flush, but not the sound of the sink.

She came back. Her hands made me shiver. I opened my eyes. "Did you wash your hands?" I asked.

"What do you think?"

They were cold, so I decided to assume she had. I lay there, the jeans still around my legs, in the same position I had been in before, as if I were tied up and couldn't move. This passivity both embarrassed me and turned me on. She took my right hand with her left and gently brought it up above my head. She held it down with her arm as she lowered her head onto my breasts and bit my right nipple.

"Ow," I moaned. But I didn't push her away. In fact, the lower part of my body gyrated towards her. She took my other hand and placed it above my head. She held both my arms down with one of hers as she crawled on top of me until her knees pinned down my arms. She pulled my belt through the loops on my jeans and wrapped it around my hands. Then she took the end and tied it around the leg of the couch.

Both the leather and buckle cut into my wrists. The belt wasn't very long and I was pulled partway off the couch. "That hurts," I said.

"But you don't mind," she said. Silence. "Do you?"

"Not exactly."

"I didn't think so." She stared at me rather impersonally, then slapped me lightly on the face.

"Ow," I said. But it didn't really hurt.

"Come on," she said. She ran her fingers very lightly down my stomach, then all of a sudden slapped me again.

This time it did hurt, but I didn't say anything. "How does that feel?" she asked.

"Okay," I said.

"Okay? Is that all? We'll have to do something about that." She slapped me again, even harder.

"*Ow.*" This time I wasn't so sure I liked it. It was no longer part of my fantasy. I wasn't sure what was coming next. For the first time I really pulled at my hands to see if I could get free.

"Roll over," she said.

"What?"

"Roll over." With the belt around my hands it was hard to do this. I had to move even more off the couch and somehow turn over without falling off. Gently she ran the tips of her fingers over my ass. It rose slightly in the air, waiting for her. Whether the goosebumps were from her touch or the cold, I didn't know. I kept worrying I would fart. She stroked down the crack to my vagina, where she soaked up some goop with her finger. She used this to lubricate my asshole.

"One sec," she said. She got up, went over to her jacket to get something out, came back. With my eyes shut I waited for her finger, or maybe even a tongue (in those days before the Plague), but I felt something hard and unfleshy feeling press against me. "You ever use one of these?" she asked.

By turning my head as much as I could, I could see the

black leather around her groin and the pink latex in the shape of a penis sticking out from it.

"Not this way," I said. "Won't it hurt?"

"That's up to you." She spread apart my cheeks and moved forward over my ass, then began to press the dildo into me.

"That hurts," I said.

"Just relax." She ran her fingers over my ass, and I felt the goosebumps again. I realized I was tensing my muscles, and told myself to let go. As I exhaled she pushed it in further.

"Ow!"

"I told you. *Relax.*" She moved a hand back inside my vagina, and in spite of the pain the wet began to flow, as if there were two separate bodies inside my one head. The other hand continued to help ease the tip of the dildo far enough into my body so that it wouldn't fall out. When I had relaxed enough to open myself to the pain, she put the hand that had been holding the dildo inside my mouth. The hand smelled like wet rubber, and I liked it. She moved her fingers in and out of my mouth in a kind of lulling rhythm; I drooled on them as if it were a cock I was sucking. Then she began to move her fingers along my gums and the muscles under my tongue, even into my nose, then back into my mouth. It was strangely erotic, though I did begin to worry about germs. With all this distraction I did not have much mental space to concentrate on the area of diffuse pain around my asshole where she was still pushing in the dildo. When on occasion I thought of it I moaned, but the pain, although intense, was made bearable by the thought of my strange submission.

Not just bearable, *pleasurable*, at the thought that all my holes were filled, my body possessed, not by just anyone, but by this being who disgusted me. Had it been someone I cared about it might have been different, but since I did not know her and there was nothing I could do about it, I might as well relax and enjoy it. No doubt I would have been happy enough with her on a desert island, where she could make love to me all day and no one would ever know. And yet, with world enough and time, perhaps I would not have wanted to let her do it, or she herself might not have wanted to do it. For is it not often true, that when you want someone to make love to you all day they don't want to, so you have to make love to them in order to get them to want to make love to you—so the person who wants sex the least generally gets more of it?

Then, beyond the pain and mental pleasures, came a powerful sensation of peace. I realized all my life I'd wanted something in there. The hand that had pushed in the dildo now cupped my right breast, as if a boat had capsized and she was hanging on to me. I was tired and I wanted to go to sleep. The sweat on my body was drying up. I hadn't had an orgasm, and I knew I wouldn't get one. "I'm cold," I said.

She kissed the back of my neck, which made me shiver even more. Then she took her hands off my breast and out of my vagina and began to push herself up off my back. The dildo pulled out a little, which hurt, though not as much as when she had put it in. "Ow," I said. But what I really felt was sadness. I had gotten used to it in there.

"Shh." She fiddled with something, then abruptly stood up. The peaceful sensation was still inside my body, but less so. When I turned my head I saw that the dildo was no longer attached to the black leather belt. She untied the end of my belt from the couch leg and lifted me up. "Be careful," I said. She was small and I was scared she'd drop me.

She carried me perhaps fifteen feet to my bed and laid me gently down. The belt was still looped around my hands and my ass still had the dildo sticking out of it. She took a blanket and placed it over me. It pressed down on the dildo a little, which felt good.

Then she crawled on top of me, turned my head to the side, and kissed me. Her lips were incredibly soft, and in spite of my fatigue I felt sexual stirrings again. "What can I do for you?" I asked. I wanted to bury my head in her, in order to fall asleep.

"Nothing."

"You sure?"

She kissed me again, then stood up and began to walk away. Again I shut my eyes. I wondered what other trick she was going to come back with—blindfold, handcuffs, tit clamps.

"Goodbye," she said.

"What?" I opened my eyes. She was standing by the bed, buttoning up her jacket.

"I got to split. You know. Diane."

Tears rushed to my eyes. Whether it was because I didn't want her to go, or because I didn't want the peaceful sensation that had spread from my asshole to the rest of my body to leave, I couldn't be sure. I began to imagine my loneliness after she'd gone. "I give the best head in the world," I said. "Haven't you heard?"

"So *that's* who they were talking about in the bar." She was so deadpan that for a moment I got paranoid. I never expected anybody I was with to have the slightest sense of humor.

"I really do," I said.

"Some other time."

She moved towards me, and I waited for her to remove the dildo. Instead, she pushed it in further.

"Ow."

"That's in pretty good now, isn't it?" She patted it.

"Yes."

"I'm going to leave you like this."

"No. It *hurts.*" But the more it hurt, the more I liked it. And her, standing calmly by in her jacket, indifferently pushing the pink latex into me.

"You really don't mind, do you?" Silence. "Do you?"

"I guess not," I admitted.

"I knew you wouldn't." She gave a last shove, then bent down to kiss me quickly on the mouth. Then she headed for the door.

I knew it could be dangerous to be left like this, my arms still tied by my belt, but I didn't protest.

"Will you come back to get it?" I asked.

"Maybe. You never know." She opened the door, then left. The words "I love you" played through my mind, although I knew they weren't true. But I felt as sad as if they were true. For a while I lay there, then I maneuvered the belt off my hands, pulled out the dildo, and went into the bathroom to brush my teeth and wash my face. Even when I was back in bed, listening to the country music station play songs from a region I wished I had been able to escape from rather than move towards, as I was doing now, the sadness stayed with me. It was the same sadness that was always there, and it occurred to me I must like it. Why else did I keep going to the bars, if not to find it?

epilog: 1988

The apartment I used to live in looked out on the river, and I would sit on the window seat and stare at the men parading past each other, some alone, some walking their dogs, some with huge ghetto-blasters which turned the promenade into a disco. In the summer they would take off their shirts and I would see muscles freshly sculpted in a bodybuilding gym burst out of bikini shorts or cut-off jeans; in the winter the light from a briefly opened car door would illuminate their snow-covered faces as if I were watching a TV screen clouded with static, and either way I would envy the careless insouciance of their lust and the easy accommodation of their desires.

Across from me was that broken-down old pier where

men held their secret assignations. I would sometimes wander there with my friend Cam, marveling at the way the sunlight fell in broken stripes through half-rotted ceilings and walls onto collapsing floorboards through which one could occasionally glimpse the river. In these ruined choirs illumined by horizontal shafts of late afternoon sun where you could see the dust beams dance, the quiet broken only by the groaning of floorboards and men, the unzipping of a zipper, the occasional smack of hand or belt across a body, I would feel I was in some unholy cathedral, one in which the scent was of marijuana and poppers rather than incense, the offering not wine and wafers but the white droppings of birds and men: the latter of which was absorbed by kneeling bodies in a mystic transformation of Idea into Flesh. And how could anyone know that amidst the dark, warm, moist lushness of herpes, clap, amebiasis, hepatitis, syphilis, crabs, etc., other transformations were taking place too? And following Cam, who would stop with nose upturned like a hunting dog as he spied his prey, I would strut across the floor, fingers hooked inside the pockets of my faded jeans, my eyes narrowed to a slit as if I were James Dean, a cowboy coming off a dusty plain, a sailor back from a sea that burned fire into one's eyes like the setting sun over New Jersey—or the orange windows in the brick warehouse across the street which reflected the sun back into my mirrored sunglasses, which of course reflected them back again . . . And in the immense power of my imagination I would envy the calm purity of utter degradation, and curse the slowness, the laziness, the inefficiency, the cowardice and hypocrisy of women—so desirous of the amenities of conversation and a nice clean bed, a history for a face that would somehow provide Romantic justification for that utterly simple desire to explore the wet insides of another's body. For I had taken the promise of our liberation seriously, and thought that, with the right attitude, anybody could be perceived as the most desirable in the world—at least for one night. That was the only way I could bring myself to desire someone—if she was the most desirable person in the world. And I would wonder if I were really not something else entirely, a man in a woman's body, perhaps, a redneck man in a woman's body, or maybe something even worse—a man who liked to fuck men in a woman's body; that is, a man in a woman's body who fucked women because this was the closest a man who was a woman could come to being a homosexual. And I would stay there as twilight fell, as the lights across the water came on in a thousand houses and cars, the latter bobbing like buoys as they floated around such obstacles as trees and houses, and around me also would appear the burning tips of a hundred cigarettes, lit by men in the way of airports—less for illumination than destination—and I would wonder where my port was, and if I was ever coming home.

Now the baths are closed, the pier has long since been torn down, and with the revelers of those bright days so too my envy has gone. Hot nights for men now consist of circle jerks; many of the former "sluts" are chaste. I myself, as the song says, don't get around much any more.

One night after a party I found myself in front of the Boxcar. As far as I know, I expected nothing, but I walked inside. Since Brett had defected to Miami I couldn't count on anybody I knew being there, and nobody I knew was there. Nobody knew I was there either; nobody knew who

I was; nobody even looked at me. Although inside I was still sixteen, a bratty adolescent, the mirror over the bar told me I was the age of the women I used to scorn, so perhaps it was only fitting that young girls raced their eyes past mine as I used to race mine past those of older women years ago. Back then I imagined I saw pools of misery spreading from them, but if that's what anybody saw now they were wrong. It was not misery but astonishment, at the person I had been and the person I was now.

The person I was now could not remember the person I had been. I thought if I could remember the women I had been with then this might help me remember the woman who had been with them—the woman who was me—but I could not remember them. That is, even if I could picture their faces, they were no more familiar to me than if I had only seen them in a bar—or perhaps only imagined seeing them. I realized (or perhaps remembered, for surely it was not the first time I had had this thought) that even when I had been with them what I had really been doing was imagining them. Now I could not even imagine imagining them. It was as if it all had not happened, or was familiar, not in the way of life, but in the way of some old movie, nostalgic, and somehow lacking all connection with "reality." Yet, of all things it had once been the most real. And I had no idea why it was different now. If I was different it was not so much that I was different but that I had had the same thoughts for so long that the sheer weight of them might perhaps now be seen to have made a difference.

I knew the way I was thinking was bullshit, yet it felt very profound, as what I thought in the bar always felt profound, perhaps because it was not a normal place to be. Or rather, it was normal for me, but not for everybody else. But now it seemed odd that for all these years it had seemed so normal. I had come to the bar for knowledge, but it turned out that that knowledge was only about how to behave in bars such as this. Now that I had that knowledge I was too old to use it—or maybe it was only that I was too old to want to use it.

It didn't seem fair. I couldn't tell you how many times I have had that thought—about things such as this and others perhaps even more important.

The girls marched towards each other, staggered around drunk, clutched each other on the dance floor. I guess, in a sense, they were beautiful, but the kind of beauty they had repelled me. It was a beauty of youth, an innocence disguised by red lipstick and odd haircuts and iconographically proper clothing that nonetheless revealed a kind of innocence different from the one they were attempting to conceal, and this was an innocence that was willed rather than real, and for that reason was doubly disgusting. I had never possessed any of the forms of innocence, so of course I envied them this. Nonetheless I did not want to be them, and when I asked myself if, in all honesty, I wanted to want to be them, I decided I did not want that either.

I still wanted something, of course, but what it was was more ineffable than ever.

A woman walked over and smiled at me. She was what in more innocent days I would have considered an attractive woman, and yet I turned my head and ordered a beer.

I watched for a while—as I would have the natives of New Guinea or a married couple in Passaic, New Jersey—then I left the bar and walked over to Sheridan Square. The men were with each other and their dogs, and the women were hugging each other against the cars, and from the straights I heard such things as "Paradise Island" and "Montego Bay." In the absence of desire or envy I felt scarcely human, and this, at least, was familiar, so that I felt like myself, after all, as I paid for the *Times* and stood in the street competing with couples for my solitary cab home. For a moment I wondered reflexively what they thought of me, these hideous familial units contemplating the subversive solitary being; then I realized I no longer cared. I did not hate them and I did not love them, and it occurred to me that perhaps they did not love or hate me either, that all along they had been merely indifferent, as I had been to those in the world who for various reasons I had decided did not count. This list included almost everybody, and to think of myself on it should have been upsetting, but it wasn't—perhaps because I had always known that in some sense I did not "count"—and this had to do with nothing so simple as whether I was alone or with someone else. When I was in a room by myself there was no one in it, which is why there had to be noise: the TV, the radio, a phone call—or two or even three of the above. Sometimes I would go to turn on the radio and it would already be on, and sometimes, while reading the newspaper, I would look around for something to read. On occasion, when I fell in love, someone was with me in the room and it was no longer empty, but quickly they became part of the furniture, the television, the paint on the walls, and the papers on my desk.

This disturbed me, of course, but in the immense vanity of my self-love and self-hate it was just one more way in which I managed to prove to myself and whoever was listening that I was the most incredible human being in the entire world.

about the author

Jane DeLynn is a playwright, journalist, and
librettist as well as the author of the critically
acclaimed novels *Real Estate, In Thrall,* and *Some
Do.*